SOME OF TIM'S STORIES

Oklahoma Stories & Storytellers

Teresa Miller, Series Editor

SOME OF TIM'S STORIES

S. E. Hinton

UNIVERSITY OF OKLAHOMA PRESS : NORMAN

The stories in Part 1 of this book are works of fiction. Names, characters, places, and incidents are either the product of the author's imagination or are used fictitiously, and any resemblance to actual events, locales, or persons, living or dead, is entirely coincidental.

Library of Congress Cataloging-in-Publication Data

Hinton, S. E.
  Some of Tim's stories / S. E. Hinton.
    p. cm. — (The Oklahoma stories & storytellers series ; v. 2)
  2nd half of the book is interviews with the author.
  ISBN 978-0-8061-3835-0 (hardcover : alk. paper)
  1. Oklahoma — Fiction.
  2. Hinton, S. E. — Interviews.
  I. Title.
  PS3558.I548S66 2007
  813'.54 — dc22
                          2006033610

Some of Tim's Stories is volume 2 in the Oklahoma Stories & Storytellers series.

1 2 3 4 5 6 7 8 9 10

To David
Who never seemed to mind
when Tim dropped by

I want to thank my friend Teresa Miller
for all her hard work
in making this book possible.

CONTENTS

SOME OF TIM'S STORIES

The Missed Trip   3
Full Moon Birthday   7
Different Shorelines   12
The Will   17
What's Your Poison?   20
The Girl Who Loved Movies   25
Sentenced   29
After the Party   36
Jailed   41
Class Time   46
Visit   50
The Sweetest Sound   54
Homecoming   58
No White Light No Tunnel   63

INTERVIEWS WITH S. E. HINTON

Conducted by Teresa Miller

The Outsiders   71
Sequels   89
Movies   105
Little Kids and Vampires   121
Tim   137

SOME OF TIM'S STORIES

THE MISSED TRIP

"Not till you're twelve. That's the rule," Uncle TJ said.

"That's a dumb rule," Terry said. "That's two more years."

Mike didn't say anything, knowing it was useless, but Terry never took a "no" he didn't have to.

"At least you guys will get to go together." Mike's dad loaded the last of the camping gear and guns into the car. "Think how poor TJ felt, getting left behind for four years, seeing me and Grandpa and Great-uncle Jack go off without him. He even stowed away in the trunk one year. When Grandpa found him, we were a hundred miles out, and he turned right around and brought him home."

"And he blistered my butt besides," Uncle TJ said. He rubbed Terry's head. "Two more years, pal."

"Well, you two ready to go live off the land?" Mom and her sister, Aunt Jelly, came out of the house.

When the men left, the moms would joke for days about them "living off the land."

"They stop at Safeway, the meat market, and the liquor store before they leave city limits," they laughed.

The boys knew better. Still, there were probably secrets to this trip their dads made every year, sometimes for a long weekend, sometimes for a week. They never missed it. The men had gone deer hunting in October every year since they were twelve years old. Only missed the years Mike's dad was off to war.

The boys knew they were supposed to continue this, and someday bring their kids, too. When those kids were twelve.

The trip was supposed to mean something. Mark something. It wasn't just the deer hunting, or the first driving lessons Terry was so crazy for. . . .

Mike's dad kneeled down and said, "Don't be too anxious for this, Michael. It's the beginning of the end of childhood. That's exciting, but a little sad."

Mike was ashamed to think he didn't want to grow up too fast, not like Terry who was always grabbing at things out of reach.

This childhood seemed perfect to him: the two families mixed together, two brothers who had married two sisters, his cousin who was more his twin.

It was like having two dads, two men who didn't just give them balls and bats but played along with them, who preferred the boys to fishing buddies on long trips to the lake, who taught them to water ski and handle guns and helped them mow the yards.

But each boy loved his own dad best. Mike couldn't understand how you could talk about anything serious with Uncle TJ, who had a joke for anything. . . .

Terry couldn't see the pleasure Mike found in silent hours with his father, sitting in a boat or in a duck blind.

"Me and Terry can sometimes feel what the other one is thinking," Mike told his dad once.

His dad said, "Yes. We could see that even when you were babies."

Uncle TJ would have started his long story about the moms wanting twins but not wanting to be pregnant with them, so they divided the set. . . . It was a funny story and

Mike and Terry still rolled with laughter even after they no longer believed it.

But still, Mike liked his dad's answer best.

"Come on in, boys, you're going to freeze," the moms said after their hugs good-bye.

But Mike and Terry stayed to watch the car drive off.

"I can't wait," Terry said.

"It'll be better if we're ready."

In his search to find something to blame for what happened after, Mike even hoped Uncle TJ had been driving—he was a careless driver, everyone knew that. But no, there was nothing to blame except God or bad weather, and that was so useless Mike gave it up after a few years.

But in later years, when he tried to think of reasons for other things, Mike often thought if he and Terry had had this trip, things would have turned out different. This trip that was to start the end of childhood.

Maybe they wouldn't have wrecked and wasted all the gifts they had been given, like kids who couldn't understand what some things cost.

The moms had done the best they could—no blame there—Mike's step-father's resentment probably no more damaging than Terry's mom's indulgence.

But by the time the boys were twenty-five, good memories grew tainted with a sad relief that the dads never saw the sorry mess made of their hopes and cares and dreams . . .

In the darkest part of the darkest nights . . .

When Mike woke sweat-drenched, still half-drunk and more than half hungover . . .

And Terry lay listening to the snores of his cellmate, concentrating on the snores of his cellmate so he wouldn't hear the other sounds . . .

When even across two hundred miles they could feel each other's mind, trying to find something to lay blame to:

Bad company, little money, less thought

Luck and fate and choice

Reckless, careless, stupid

Remorse, regret—the only feelings left sometimes. . . .

They mostly blamed themselves, and only rarely blamed each other.

They never took that easy out, the one you heard a lot these days.

They'd had a happy childhood. It was more than most people got.

FULL MOON BIRTHDAY

"Just think," Terry said. "It's Friday the thirteenth, a full moon, and your twenty-first birthday. Anything could happen, man, just about anything."

"I know what's going to happen if you don't behave," Mike said.

Terry had been playing eye-tag with one of the four young ladies seated behind them. There were four men sitting there, too.

"Now just who is buying you your first legal drink here?"

"I haven't seen you fork over the money."

"What are you looking at, kid?" said a voice from behind them. Big guy in a hunting cap.

Mike choked on his drink when Terry answered: "Just admiring your lovely granddaughter, sir."

Surely Terry's famous luck had run out with that one. . . .

But the guy just said, "She's had enough of your admiration. And she's not my granddaughter."

Terry shrugged apologetically and turned back to the bar.

"Full moon, anything's likely to happen," he repeated. "And you got to admit this was a good idea."

He set his drink down and wandered off in the direction of the john.

Mike agreed with him there. Coming to Colorado to fish was a good idea. Different scenery, different weather. They had caught their limit and then some.

The ones you ate on the spot didn't count, Terry said.

Mike was going to start a new job in a week, on a street crew. It was nice to get a little vacation in first.

Terry had been gone for a while, Mike noticed, when he heard a chair scrape behind him, saw hunting-cap head for the john.

But instead of going in the door marked "Bucks," he kicked open the one marked "Does."

And there was the girl, sitting on the sink, her legs wrapped around Terry's waist, her arms wrapped around Terry's neck, and it was a pretty good bet she had her tongue wrapped around Terry's tongue.

Mike slapped down a bill to pay for the drinks and charged out the door, knowing Terry was so quick he'd probably beat him to the parking lot—and he almost did.

The four guys chasing them cut them off from the truck, so they ran across the road and down into the woods.

The roar of the river got louder, and Terry yelled, "Jump in and swim for it!"

Hearing the crashing through the woods behind them,

Mike thought this was as good a plan as any, and they both hit the icy water at the same time.

The river was fast, but not furious; it was likely they'd freeze before drowning. They floated and swam downstream as long as they could before crawling on shore.

"I told you, full moon," Terry said through chattering teeth as they walked down the moonlit dirt road, totally lost. "It makes things happen."

Mike, hugging himself, shivering, was too miserable to punch him.

A truck drove by, slowed.

"You boys fall in the river?" The woman was about thirty, a little weather-beaten, but pretty.

"Yes ma'am. Fishing."

"Well, you'll freeze out here at night, wet like that. You look harmless enough. Hop in." She had a low, husky voice. A kind voice. "Name's Chris."

Back at her place, she gave them some of her ex-husband's sweats to wear when they got out of the shower, while she ran their clothes through the washer and dryer. He must have been a tall guy. They fit fine.

Terry walked around, looking at the old photos on the wall. Mike sat in front of the fire. It was a nice cabin. He was glad she didn't have a TV. It was the kind of a place where you didn't want a TV.

"Great place you got here, ma'am," Terry said, when Chris came back with some beers. She was smaller than she'd seemed in the truck.

"Don't call me that, it makes me feel old. You want a tour?"

"Sure."

Mike stayed where he was, watching the fire. Twenty-one. . . .

They were gone a long time. When they came back, Terry was wearing a damn goofy grin; Chris was wearing a robe.

Mike felt a jolt like electricity when she put her hand on his hair.

"I hear it's your birthday," she said softly. . . .

The truck was still there the next morning. But their ice chest, the tackle were gone.

"Dammit!" Mike said. "That was my favorite rod."

"Could have been the tires," Terry said cheerfully. "You got to admit it turned out nice."

Almost killed, almost drowned, almost froze, but by the time Terry was through, Mike's twenty-first birthday would sound like the best one on record.

Mike glanced at the sky, the faint moon still in sight. My birthday moon. . . . Oh God, just once, let me see Terry get worried.

They stopped in Trinidad for lunch, tacos and margaritas.

"You two twins?" the waitress asked, puzzled, when she checked their IDs. They'd been asked that before—the same last name, the strong family resemblance. . . .

"Yep. Twins. But born two months apart."

"Cousins." Mike cut that story short. He was still pissed.

Terry watched another customer get up, leave.

"Weird-looking dude," he remarked.

"Or dudette." The waitress set down their drinks.

"What?"

"Trinidad's the sex-change capital of the world. We got the best nut-picking doctor in the States. You see a lot of strange-looking strangers around here. They do it in stages. But some of them turn out right pretty."

Terry shuddered violently.

"Hey." Mike was struck by a thought. "You don't think Chris? . . ."

"Dammit," Terry said desperately. "Don't even think it!"

Mike grinned to himself. He didn't think it. He wasn't the hound Terry was, but he knew a woman when he tripped over one in the dark.

"It was kind of strange, the way she had men's clothes laying around?"

"Shut up," Terry said.

Mike sipped his margarita.

"Her voice. . . ."

"Shut up." Terry's face was sweating. He looked a little green.

It was was nice to see him worried.

"You're gonna keep this up all the way back to Oklahoma," Terry accused.

"Yep." Mike ordered another round. To celebrate.

DIFFERENT SHORELINES

Mike's feet touched bottom, and he staggered onto shore.
"I won," he gasped out, falling onto the towel.

His cousin Terry dropped down beside him, panting.

"This time," Terry admitted.

Terry won the short races, Mike usually won the long.
They were like that at everything they did. Terry was quick
but couldn't pay attention for long; Mike was stubborn.

"Wonder what the suckers back in school are doing."
Terry pawed through his clothes, found the cigarettes.

Mike knew what at least a few of them were doing. History test. One he'd studied for, too.

Mike had made up his mind. He wasn't going to drop out, flunk. It would give the step-bastard too much satisfaction, the way he kept predicting something like that.

But Terry had made a lot of sense, saying today would be better for the lake. No people, no crowds. Not that *he* minded; Mike was the shy one.

Terry knew the way to get Mike to skip school. He could always read his mind. Cousins, but it must be something like having a twin, Mike thought. They were closer than most brothers.

"You want to head back now?" Terry asked.

If they left for home now, no one would know where they'd been—though it wouldn't matter much to Terry.

Aunt Jelly would believe anything he told her, or he'd sweet-talk her out of being mad in five minutes. She'd say he was grounded, but that wouldn't last long. . . .

Mike would be facing the step-bastard, who would yell a lot and then take off his belt, his mom would just watch.

"No," Mike said. "The fish will be biting after sundown. We don't want to waste bait."

"You can be a real mule, Mike," Terry said.

Mike lit his own cigarette, lay back to look at the sky.

It was a real nice day for the lake.

SUMMER 1994

"We'll get a boat," Terry said.

"What we need is a truck." Mike took a long hit off the joint and passed it back.

"Travis Fish & Ski."

Mike hadn't thought about details, but since fishing and skiing were two of his three favorite things, that brand of boat sounded fine.

"Chick magnet."

Well, there's number three, Mike thought.

"I'll tell you what, you get the truck, I'll get the boat. We'll have enough money for both in a couple of months."

Mike stared out at the lake. Boat sounded good. He felt like he was on one now, just drifting along, nice breeze. . . .

"What is your problem?" Terry asked.

"Who says I have a problem?"

"You just usually do." Terry dug around in the cooler, got out another couple of beers.

Mike didn't say anything. Even if he was stone-cold sober, Terry could talk rings around him. No use trying to argue now.

"We're not hurting anybody, Mike."

"Yes. I know."

"It's not that dangerous. We know the guys."

"Yes," Mike said again, and popped open his beer.

"We'll never get our hands on money like this."

Mike tried to hang onto his nice, fuzzy high, ignore the uneasiness in his gut.

"You know what your problem is?"

Mike said, "I worry too much."

Sometimes he thought the first words out of Terry's mouth must have been, "Mike, you worry too much."

"Well, yeah," Terry said. "That and the constant farting."

Mike choked on his laugh, his beer, and threw what was left at his cousin.

But Terry was already in the lake.

FALL 1996

"We used to bring you kids here when you were little," Aunt Jelly said.

"I remember," Mike said.

There were still some little kids determined to stay in the

water; it was likely to be the last warm weekend of the year. Already the water was cold.

"Just a little while longer?" they'd whine when their moms made them get out. Their teeth would be chattering, their lips blue, and all they could think of was getting back in.

Mike could remember whining like that. He picked up his cigarettes from the picnic table, tapped another one out.

"He says it's not as bad as you think. His cellmate is fine. They have a window."

Sometimes Mike thought Aunt Jelly must have had a stroke or something, since Terry . . . left.

She seemed so stunned. Strange. She was not a stupid woman.

Mike knew damn well there was no window.

"It's not forever."

Mike looked across the lake. It was years. Sometimes it seemed like forever to him, and he was not in there.

He looked at his truck. He was going to sell it, trade it. He'd never have a chance to get another, new, but the sight of it made his stomach turn.

The boat was gone. They took it.

The truck was in Mike's name.

"It's not your fault," Aunt Jelly said suddenly, fiercely. She put her hand on his arm. "Terry knew what he was doing. He knew the risks."

"Yes," Mike said. After all, it was the truth.

"And it's not your fault you're not in there with him."

"Just a little while longer?" the little kids whined.

They could not tell it was cold.

WINTER 1999

Mike walked along the shoreline. He should have brought his fishing tackle, he thought.

But he hadn't planned where he'd go today, just got in his old truck and drove.

He took the stick Amos brought back, and threw it as hard as he could. Then sat down on a log and stared at the water.

Forever wasn't over yet. It still had years to go.

Amos came back with the stick, dropped it. Put his head on Mike's knee and whined. He was a real quiet dog. It wasn't often he whined.

Mike stood up, zipped his jacket. It was too cold to stay. It was getting dark; he needed to go to work.

Something was his fault. He was sure about that.

THE WILL

"You didn't need to get all dressed up for this," the step-father said.

Mike looked at him but said nothing. He had come from work; he would go back to work from here. You didn't get all dressed up to work on a street crew.

His cousin Terry winked at him. Terry was dressed fine, but he was between jobs as usual and had nothing better to do.

Aunt Julie smiled at Mike. He had come to the reading of the will because she asked him to. She wouldn't care if he didn't dress up.

I hope it says something about Dad's guns, Mike thought. Because I am taking them one way or the other.

The woman who was Aunt Julie's sister, his step-father's wife, had just died.

To Mike it seemed like his mother had died a long time ago.

He was glad he went to see her in the hospital, though. Glad Terry had made him.

"You will be so sorry if you don't, man," Terry had said, and Mike was glad he had listened. He could see it meant a lot to his mother.

He held the step-father's eyes again.

I am twenty-three, not seventeen, Mike thought. Your yelling would not make me nervous now, and if you make one move to take off your belt I will strangle you with it.

Mike had thought his life was ruined when he was ten years old and Dad's car went off that icy bridge. Then two years later his mother had married this man, and Mike found out what ruined was.

The lawyer was saying something about the jewelry going to Aunt Julie. It wasn't much, but Mike was still glad she would get it and not the step-father.

He could tell Terry was trying not to laugh. He always saw the comical side to things, and this lawyer, he sounded just so damn . . . lawyery.

(But after the funeral, Terry had sat in Mike's truck with him and hugged him while they both bawled like babies.)

The lawyer was talking about the house now, the house he had grown up in, Mike heard the address. Then heard, ". . . to my son, Michael Timothy" and looked up to make sure he was hearing right.

One look at the step-father's face told him.

Of course the guy started fussing and protesting, and dimly Mike heard the lawyer saying the house had originally been Mike's father's, left to his wife and son, and yes maybe the terms could have been changed—but they weren't. In fact, she had seen the lawyer about a year ago to make sure Mike got the house.

I'll paint it back white like it is supposed to be, and Terry can get off his lazy butt and help me if he wants to move in, Mike thought. And yank up that god-awful carpet. . . .

He'd get a dog, not like Bingo, who was sent to the pound for biting the step-father, but another. . . . Yeah, he would get one from the pound, that was a good idea.

He stood up. So did the step-father.

"I have to go back to work."

He had grown a lot since he was seventeen; the other man had to look up to meet his eyes.

"She told me she changed that will," the step-father said.

"She once told me she married you because she loved you," Mike said. "Guess she lied to us both." He paused. "You got twenty-four hours to get your stuff out of my house."

Those were the exact same words he'd heard six years before, when he thought he had left that house forever.

Mike hoped the step-father remembered saying that.

"Fuck you," he started to add, but then realized Mom had said it for him.

WHAT'S YOUR POISON?

Mike had the draft in the mug before the customer sat down. He didn't know the guy's name, but he knew what he wanted. Bud draft, a package of chips. And to tell the story about the UFO.

It would take three beers, but the story would come out.

How he was driving down the highway. No drugs. No booze. No one else in the truck. The white light. The engine dying. The three things in the road. Yeah, they looked like the pictures—small, gray, a slit for a mouth, big eyes. . . . He'd passed out or something, came to on the road with a splitting headache and four hours behind schedule.

Mike would nod, listen. Give the guy what he was thirsty for.

"Yeah, that is spooky man. It would freak anyone out. Nobody could go on driving a truck after something like that. No, I never seen one, don't want to. Sounds like hell. Sure, nobody wants to go on disability, especially mental. . . ."

On the third beer the guy quit shaking, on the fourth he was talking sports.

Four beers in an evening never hurt anybody, and it was easy for Mike to do his job.

He'd worked here for three years now, since he was twenty-five and needed a steady job. It didn't pay much, but right then he didn't want much. Just something steady. He was the bouncer, too. Mike would rather keep a fight from happening than try to end one, and he was good at that. He had an eye for spotting the ones who were thirsty for a fight.

He had gotten real good at knowing what people wanted.

There was one woman, just a few years older, though sometimes, the way she carried on, you'd think she could be his mother. She didn't have any kids. Maybe that was it.

She stopped in on her way home from work. It was quiet then. Sit at the bar and order a rum and Coke.

Mike could tell which days she needed more rum than Coke.

Her arms were bruised sometimes; once or twice she had a split lip. From work, she said. She worked in an old-folks' home. It would surprise you how strong they could be. Violent.

Mike would set her drink down and hear about the old people, the mean ones, the sweet ones, the families who visited, the ones who didn't.

Then she'd say she had to get home, hubby would be worried, mad, haha, you know how men are.

Mike knew how some men were, so he would nod.

One weekend when he visited his aunt, he got the name of some agency, some place you could call when hubby got mad like that. His aunt had a friend who had been in trouble.

"What'd ya give me this for?" the customer spat at him when he gave her the number. "I don't need that."

She gulped down her drink and left. Mike felt bad. He wasn't a damn social worker. That wasn't his job.

So next time, when she came in, he acted like nothing had happened. Poured the rum and Coke.

And when she asked for a third, he said, "Maybe you better get on home. Your husband might be worried. Men lose their tempers quick, sometimes, when they get worried."

She brightened up at that.

"Yeah, it's funny, the way it takes you sometimes. Love."

Mike nodded, and she left happy. That was his job. Give them what they were thirsty for.

The guy who had fits about his daughter. Seeing the frigging therapist. They hypnotized you these days, made you say whatever they wanted. You couldn't believe the garbage, the filth—and they had the poor kid believing she really remembered....

It just broke his heart.

His wife's, too.

Mike said, "It's a shame the way people can mess with your mind."

Gave him another Jack Daniel's. His money was as green as anyone else's, even if he did give Mike the creeps.

Ed, the other bartender, never said much while they worked. Ed was a lot older. There wasn't much in common outside of the job. Once, half-kidding, Mike told him, "My name is not Fool Kid."

And Ed said, "You seem to think it is your job description." And he wasn't kidding a bit.

But after the bar was closed, when they were cleaning up, Ed would say a few things. Women. How rotten they were. He ought to know; he was married four times. They just made your life hell.

Mike said, "If you quit marrying them, maybe you would like them better. Nothing wrong with a lady friend."

And Ed would scowl, mumble. Then mention, there was this gal he'd seen at church. . . . She did seem nice. . . .

Mike said everyone could use a friend.

Mike wasn't any talker. But he could listen good. It was like he could hear a whole other conversation under the words they said. The stories—the wife, the boss, the brother-in-law, the goddamn cops. . . .

Sometimes, late Saturday nights, when he worked till 2:00, Mike would take a few tips, buy himself a couple of shots of whiskey. He could still work fine—watched out for fights, ladies who needed an escort to their cars, glasses needing to be refilled, cleaned.

Which words they wanted to hear.

Three years here.

It didn't seem that long. Saturday nights, late, the bar was so full of smoke it was like a heavy fog; the music and noise had melted together where you couldn't tell which was which, it was like being in a dream.

It was a good job, far away from that mess he and Terry got in. The paycheck didn't bounce.

Besides, he didn't know what else to do.

But he couldn't help thinking how this place would look twenty years from now. . . .

His mind went strange places that late at night. He'd have another whiskey. But it wasn't what he was thirsty for.

THE GIRL WHO LOVED MOVIES

It wasn't the first thing he thought of when he remembered her, but it had to be the second.

How much she loved movies.

Not the new ones, the ones you saw on the big screen, at least not often. Most of the new ones she scorned.

"That is so clichéd," she'd say, yawning while the rest gasped in horror, laughing when others wept.

These were the only times he ever heard her say anything harsh. She was unnaturally kind.

But she loved the old ones.

They went in together to buy a VCR, rented movies instead. Neither one of them had any money, it was cheaper.

Stretched out on the couch, Sunday afternoons in particular, they'd watch for hours.

She knew all of the actors.

"You'll never believe who was up for this part," she'd tell him. "It would have ruined the whole thing. Casting is really important."

He'd nod, not paying attention, thinking it odd how one girl's head on your shoulder, one girl's arm on your chest, one girl's leg wrapped around your leg was just a better fit than any other's.

She loved black and white.

"Look at the shadows," she said. "Color would spoil it."

He liked colors, so instead he'd look at the top of her head, the twenty shades of gold and brown it took to come up with her hair, the natural pink of her nails . . . notice that when she wore one of his T-shirts it was always the green one. . . .

"They did such a good job on lighting."

And he'd see how the sunlight lit the hairs on her arms into silver; he'd just have to stroke them. . . . How rain brought out the depth of her eyes.

"Listen to this," she said. "This line is classic."

"So what's the difference," he'd ask, not really caring, "between classic and cliché?"

"Cliché is just the same old way to say something. Anyone can mouth a cliché. Classic is taking something everyone feels and putting it so true, so different, so right, it's the best way anyone could say it."

So he learned some classic lines:

"Here's looking at you, kid."

"We'll always have Paris."

"You know how to whistle don't you? Just put your lips together and blow."

She knew how movies were made, which ones were adapted, which were written from scratch. She talked about conferences, backstory, and improv. The most important part of a movie, she told him, was story. Most of the new ones didn't have story.

He would think of their story, how they had met.

He worked on a street crew; they were repairing a neighborhood road. It was a hundred degrees, and the men were surly and mean.

And she came out of a house with a pitcher of lemonade and real glasses—like she wasn't afraid of their germs.

And she passed it around, with thanks for their work. It was the first time that happened.

You could tell she wasn't afraid they'd say rough things, get nasty. And nobody did.

When she looked at them, she looked under grime and saw people. She had those kind of eyes.

And when he went back later, clean, nervous, cursing himself for a fool, and knocked on the door—she was the babysitter, he found out—she could still see him. She didn't mistake shy for sullen or take lack of words for no thought. It was the first time anyone had seen him that clearly.

Women usually saw what he could be; this was the first who loved what he was.

It surprised him, much later, to find out how much he knew about movies. Who Alan Smithee was and what POV stood for, the difference between a medium and a long shot. It made him think about other things he'd learned from her: how to start trusting again, what a useless thing a grudge was, how to see people when you look at them. To look for the backstory.

No, she didn't mind the sad endings, though they did make her sad. It happened, she said. That was why good movies were real life. . . .

So that was always the second thing he thought of when he remembered her. How much she loved movies. . . .

But the first . . . the first was always:

I miss you.

I need you.

I love you.

I should have never let you go.

It was cliché, he knew. But he meant it classic.

SENTENCED

"He looks good," Aunt Jelly said. "Better than you'd think. Too thin, maybe, but he says the food's not great."

Mike hadn't supposed the food was great.

"He wants to know if you're getting his letters. He says he hasn't heard from you."

"Yeah I get them. But you know I'm not much on letter-writing."

What was he supposed to say? "Dear Terry, how are you? Having fun in that place? I am walking around free as a bird while you have years to go"?

But he'd get mail from Terry anyway. Every week or so.

"Dear Mike," he wrote once, "too bad you're not in here with me. We young guys are real popular."

Mike never showed his letters to Aunt Jelly. They were different from the ones she got.

"There's good things about this place, cuz," he wrote once. "After a couple of weeks you can smuggle watermelons."

Mike had crumpled that one up and slammed it into the trash. And the last one. Full of sick jokes and fake cheerfulness. Then one line, after his signature, so different and shaky you wouldn't know it for Terry's handwriting: "I am not going to make it, Mike."

And he'd spilled something on it. Or cried.

Oh God.

"I told him you'd come up to visit with me sometime." Aunt Jelly made that drive every Saturday. Four hours there, four back.

"I work late Fridays and Saturdays," Mike said. "Sometimes I don't get home till four or five."

He didn't want to know what that place looked like. He didn't want to set foot inside the doors. He'd never be able to forget the smell, he knew it.

Aunt Jelly put the bacon-and-tomato sandwich in front of him. She had lathered on the mayonnaise the way he liked it. But no onions. Terry was the one who liked onions.

Then she got the ice teas and sat across from him.

Mike looked away. Her eyes were the same color as Terry's. Kind of brown and green mixed up.

Through the back screen door he could see the tomato plants straining at the stakes, full of green and light tan fruit.

He and Terry always bitched about that when they were kids, having to dig up that garden every spring. Funny, they didn't mind it so much when they were older. Probably because they could think about the sandwiches they'd be getting, instead of how they could be playing ball.

Last spring, and this spring, Mike had done it alone, and set the plants out, too.

"Well, maybe sometime when you get a night off."

"Sure," Mike said. He took a bite. Terry loved these things, with the tomatoes right off the vine. He'd eat a half-dozen easy, if Aunt Jelly would keep frying bacon.

The bite stuck in his throat, and he washed it down with tea. He could get through one sandwich this way, but she had left the bacon out, expecting him to eat three at least.

You two eat like horses for such skinny boys. They had heard that all their lives. Then they hit twenty and filled out, like someone had colored in an outline, and people said no wonder you two ate so much.

Mike wondered what Terry was eating this afternoon. Maybe they got something special on Sundays.

He put his sandwich down.

"I saw Amber at Dillard's. She said to say hi."

"I don't need to hear from her," Mike said. "We've been broke up a year."

"Well," said Aunt Jelly.

That last night he spent with Amber. Starting off sweet and slow like always, getting hotter and fiercer. He was settling on top of her, and then he had to go and think, "Terry can't do this."

And then think what Terry might be doing instead. He lost it fast, like he'd heard you could, but it was the first time for him.

The feel of someone else's skin on his had made him sick; he had the flu, he told her, after he ran to the john to puke. And sure enough, he shook all night with chills.

He got drunk, picked a fight with Amber the next day, scared if he tried to get close to her again it would happen just the same. And the day after that. It surprised him how long she stayed with him. But she had finally left.

"So any new girl, then?"

"Maybe." Mike didn't mean to sound so rude. He had always loved talking to Aunt Jelly. Sometimes even more than to his own mom. Especially after the step-bastard. He had spent a lot of time at this house after the step-bastard.

But it was hard to talk to her now. The room felt so empty without Terry.

Mike shook himself like a wet dog. He had to quit thinking like this. He'd go nuts if this kept up.

Last Thursday, at the ballpark, high up in the stands, he got to thinking how when they were little, they'd come up here to drop peanuts on people. Then in high school, to cruise for girls. Then, the last few years, to watch the game.

When the crowd got up and left, Mike did too. He had no idea of the score.

"So what are you doing the rest of the day?" Aunt Jelly asked. She had seen it was no use making another sandwich.

"Change the oil in the truck," Mike said. "Next week I'll do yours."

He looked after her car now, but even before he'd done most of it. Terry'd hang around and talk while Mike did most of the work. Mike didn't mind; Terry was a good talker.

Holy shit. Was he never going to quit thinking this way? It had been over a year now.

He couldn't lay in the grass and look up at the sky and not think, "Terry can't do this."

He couldn't go fishing, play catch with the dog, stop

in the grocery store, take a nice long hot shower without thinking, "Terry can't do this."

He got up and carried his plate and glass to the sink.

In the distance, a police siren wailed. The glass broke in the sink.

Aunt Jelly said, "Never mind, honey."

But Mike didn't hear.

He was back in that deserted parking lot. It was real late at night. He and Terry sat in the dark car, smoking.

"They're late," Mike said.

They were messing with stuff they shouldn't have been messing with. Dealing with people they shouldn't have been dealing with.

They knew better. They were smarter than that. All the stuff he heard later, it was true. It didn't change a thing. . . .

"Aw, they'll show up. They just better have all the money this time," Terry said.

They weren't too nervous. After four or five times you got used to thinking nothing would go wrong.

Through the alley, across the street, you could see the lights of an all-night Jiffy Stop.

"I'm going to get a slurpie," Mike said. "I'll be right back."

"Well hurry. Get me a beer while you're at it." Terry said. "Slurpie? Geez, Mike, how can you drink that shit?"

Mike got impatient with the clerk behind the counter. It wasn't like he had all night. A beer and a grape slurpie, how long could that take to ring up?

The clerk was watching TV. Columbo was about to nail the murderer. And then the screen was filled with a radar map and some weather guy blithering about tornadoes.

"Goddammit!" The clerk pounded on the counter. Then

he looked at Mike. Then past Mike's shoulder. "What's going on over there?"

There were flashing lights behind the building across the street. You could see them down the alleyway. Now there were more flashing lights coming down the street. And then they turned on the sirens.

Mike and the clerk and the two other customers watched out the glass storefront. Someone said fight. Someone said mugging. The clerk said probably a drug bust; there was so much of that around here.

Mike drank his slurpie without saying anything. When the others left, he did too.

And when the police showed up to question him the next day, he said he'd been home all night. Watching TV. *Columbo*. But the goddamn weatherman had ruined the whole thing.

That fit with Terry's story, that he'd been alone. And even though Mike could have read *Columbo*'s plot in the *TV Guide*, he wouldn't have known about the weather bulletin.

If he had been anywhere near the drug bust.

Mike couldn't bring himself to go to the trial, see Terry all scrubbed up and in that suit he'd bought only a couple of months before, for Grandma's funeral. To have Terry see him walking around free.

But he heard about the sentence. The fucking gun in the car added three more years. He had told Terry they didn't need a gun in the car. Stupidass bastard.

He stared out the kitchen window at the mimosa tree in full bloom. It was a lot bigger now than when they were kids. It smelled so strong.

"I love that smell," Terry had said. "That is pure-dee summer."

Aunt Jelly gently pushed him aside, picked the glass pieces out of the sink and put them in the trash. She wiped her hands on a towel.

She hugged him for a minute.

"It's such a comfort to me," she said, "to know, at least, *you're* free."

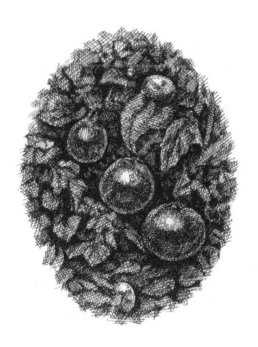

AFTER THE PARTY

"Just want to say thanks for the great party."

The female voice in Mike's ear woke him up. He'd only been half-asleep, though, with those weird dreams mixed with memories you get when sleeping drunk. He looked toward the door and saw that it was shut.

"What time is it?"

"Close to noon."

"People still here?"

"A few. Couple passed out in the other room. Some having breakfast. Cody's asleep on the couch."

"He still got his virtue?" Mike yawned.

"Still."

Mike's chuckle made his headache worse. About halfway through the night before it became obvious a few of poor

Cody's old girlfriends were going to give the groom-to-be one more try. The result was Cody appearing with a combination lock hung through his belt buckle.

Mike, headache or not, couldn't help laughing at the memory of Cody's drunken declaration: "Only Angela has my numbers. The rest of you ladies stand back."

Good party. Damn great party.

In a minute he sighed.

"You got a nice way of saying thank you."

"Bet you have a nice way to say you're welcome."

It was close to three in the afternoon when he woke up next. As bad as he wanted a beer, he had to get his teeth brushed, cold water on his face. He shook his head at the sight of his reflection. It had "good party" stamped all over it.

Someone had made an effort to clean things up—some of the dishes were washed. Had to be the girls. Mike couldn't remember one of his buddies ever tossing an empty in the trash can. Where was the chili? There had been more than enough. Someone had put it in the fridge, still in the pan. He took it out and set it on the stove, took the leftover baked potatoes out of the oven, threw them in a pot with some water to heat.

There were still a few cars in the driveway, but the only person he found in the house was Cody, sitting up now, staring blankly at a soundless basketball game. Mike sat down and handed him a cold beer.

"Where's the rest of them?"

"I think in Bill's camper. They decided it'd be better than the floor." Cody sipped his beer automatically.

"The cops were here, right?" he asked after a while.

"Twice." Mike said. "First for the music being too loud, then Starla was running around screaming her head off in the back yard. I think the neighbors thought she was being attacked."

Cody shook his head. "I take it nobody was arrested."

"It was pretty clear everything was consensual," Mike said. "But they said if they had to come back again, they'd be taking people with them. At least it got quieted down."

Mike went back to the kitchen. He couldn't stand the noise of the mixer, so he mashed the potatoes by hand, adding cheddar cheese and a small jar of jalapeños. Then he fixed two plates with mashed potatoes covered with chili and took them back to the couch.

They ate and stared at the game.

"You sure there wasn't any film in that camera?"

One of the girls who was losing at poker had hopped onto Cody's lap. Mike whipped out his camera and shot off a half-dozen flashes. He had enjoyed Cody's misery for at least an hour before he confessed to no film.

"I'm sure." Mike heard the cars starting up in the driveway. In a few minutes Bill's camper pulled out too.

"Great party," Cody said. Mike was glad he thought so. In the beginning poor Cody had been so worried Angela would find out, show up, he couldn't have any fun. And some of the teasing had bordered on mean. . . .

"It'll be the last one like that I'll have," Cody said. "Short leash from now on."

"Yes."

Mike's heartbeat picked up a little at the thought of the wedding. He ran over his list in his mind. Got the tux rented. Made sure the other guys did, too. Had Cody's plane tickets and confirmation numbers in a safe place. Would get the ring, the license from him the day before. Had part of the toast written down. . . . Just knew it'd sound stupid. . . .

"Good stripper," Cody mused.

"Ought to be at that price."

"Probably my last stripper."

Poor Cody. . . .

Mike went for a couple more beers. Somebody's shirt was on the porch. Yes, he remembered now. Bill had fallen down, landed in dog shit, chasing Starla around the yard. That was when she was screaming so loud the neighbors got worried. Guess they couldn't tell she was laughing. Damn great party. . . .

Mike tried to get interested in the basketball game but didn't even care who was playing.

"You nervous?"

"Not really," Cody said.

"You sure? No more parties. . . ."

"You remember grade school, Mike? Playing war? Then that wasn't so much fun. Then middle school, we got so serious about baseball. Then cars. . . . You just keep happening into different kinds of fun. Being married just seems like the most fun thing I can think of right now. The kind of fun that can last damn near forever."

Cody's phone started ringing, and he dug his jacket out from under the sofa cushions to answer.

"Hi, sweet thing. Nothing. Just over at Mike's watching the game. You have a nice time at your grandma's? Dinner at your parents? Sure. Pick you up about seven? Sure, honey. Loveya too."

Cody put the phone back in the jacket.

"You're whipped, man," Mike said.

"Yep." Cody took another pull on his beer. "Your turn next, bud."

"Not a snowball chance."

"Poor Mike."

Cody got a damn goofy grin on his face. You could tell it wasn't from remembering the party.

JAILED

"I told you I couldn't pay you back till tomorrow."

Mike unlocked his door. He had been real surprised to see the other bartender, Ed, waiting on his front porch when he drove up. He couldn't figure out what the older man would be doing there.

"I didn't come for my money," Ed said. "I told you, no hurry."

He followed Mike into his house without an invitation, set a box down on the coffee table.

"You got to quit running around like a chicken with its head off."

"What?" Mike's nerves were humming, his temper short—he hadn't slept in three days. Yes, he owed Ed big time right now, but also he was in a really bad mood right now. The guy had better start making sense.

"You went back to the bar, didn't you? To act it out."

Mike stopped pacing for a second. That was where he had been. But the closed, deserted bar had provided no answers.

"Sit down," Ed said. "Breathe."

"What the . . . I am breathing."

"No, you're not. Sit down. Think about it. In. Out."

Mike, too buzzed to argue, sat down, took a breath. Then another. Then another. His mind cleared a little. His heartbeat slowed. He breathed.

Ed came out of the kitchen carrying two glasses. One was water. He handed it to Mike, who drank it without protest. The other was an ice tea glass full of whiskey, and he handed that to Mike too.

"I will kill the next cop who tries to cuff me," Mike said after a long swallow.

He looked at the marks on his wrists. There had been no need for that. He wasn't resisting arrest.

"I don't think so." Ed sat in a chair across the table, opened the box. It was pizza.

"I'm not hungry."

"You're starved," Ed said.

Mike was getting tired of this. Ed always treated him like a kid. Even called him that most of the time.

"I won't go back to jail."

"You won't have to. Not for this. The guy is going to cool off, drop charges. You get paid for throwing jerks out of the bar; you were just doing your job. He swung first. There's a dozen witnesses. You won't even get a fine."

Mike slugged some more whiskey. He had been real surprised to see the cops come into the bar. It wasn't a normal occurrence. More surprised when they cuffed him, shoved him into the back seat. Surprised at his own violent reaction.

If he hadn't been cuffed, they couldn't have shoved him around. He had yanked at the cuffs, making them tighter.

"Hang on, kid." From somewhere he had heard Ed's voice. "I'll get you out. Hang on."

Mike's heart had pounded. A rage flickered. He couldn't remember being helpless like this.

"Open a window, willya?" he had said at last. The cops paid no attention, and Mike didn't repeat his request.

If he could have gotten the cuffs off, he would have killed them. He knew it.

"Look," Ed said now. "I've watched you bounce bozos outta the bar for three years. I've never seen you do anything you'd serve time for. You sometimes drive when you shouldn't, that'll do it, too. But you're good at your job. Don't worry."

Mike was remembering being in the cell. The other guys hadn't bothered him; he wasn't the first person you'd pick to mess with. But he could not breathe in that place. He looked at his watch every two minutes, sure that hours had passed. He'd paced back and forth, like a dog on a chain.

He would have skinned himself live to get out of that place.

He was halfway through his whiskey. He finally admitted what was on his mind.

"Other guys get jailed. Do time. Laugh about it. I shouldn't have freaked out like that."

"You're claustrophobic, kid. You know that."

Mike hadn't thought about it. But it was true he always had to have a window open, in a car, in a house, no matter what weather, had to work the window end of the bar. He could not get into an elevator, but Saturday night he'd been shoved into one anyway. . . .

The pizza was half gone. He drank some more whiskey.

"Terry. . . ." he said.

"Yeah, cousin Terry's doing hard time, and you should be in there with him."

Mike looked up.

"You talk more than you think when you're drinking. And you sure as hell drink more than you know."

"If I was in there with him maybe we could watch each other's back or something."

"I doubt it. You'd be in the nut bin by now. He like you?"

Mike was puzzled. They were the same age, had the same long-boned build, the same color of hair. People always took them for brothers. . . .

"I mean with this claustrophobia thing."

"No."

Terry was bad about heights. Mike did not know if there were any heights in that place.

He never went to see.

Mike wondered what it would be like to wake up in the morning and not wonder, first thing, if Terry was still alive.

"Well, he may come out of it okay. Some of them do. I did a year in a county jail. It was a piece of cake after 'Nam. Take off your boots."

"Why?"

"You're going to pass out in five minutes, and I don't want to do it for you."

It was hotter than hell when he woke up. It had been one of those stifling Oklahoma nights. Must be in the nineties. Was the air conditioner out? No, the small window unit was still pumping out cold.

Then he knew, without looking, that all the windows, both doors were open. It had happened before. Sometimes he even remembered doing it.

Mike rolled to sit up, rubbed his head. He was so sick of hangovers. . . .

He wondered if Terry was still alive.

CLASS TIME

Mike watched the teacher walk back and forth in front of the blackboard. She was a little thing, maybe five-three or -four, barely came up to his shoulder. She looked to be about twenty-five, a couple of years younger than he was.

He had expected to be the oldest one in this American Short Stories class, but there were several students far older than he was. Just a few looked fresh out of high school. It had been almost ten years since he'd been in high school. And he sure didn't remember any teachers that looked like this.

Once in a while she would stop, look down at her notes on her desk. When she did this, a piece of hair would fall forward over her face, and she would absent-mindedly brush it back behind her ear.

Mike kept thinking he would like to smooth her hair back like that. She had pretty, light brown hair, a gleam like silk to it.

He should be paying attention to what she was saying. Something about Henry James. He hadn't been able to read the Henry James story, though he did like the one by Hemingway. . . .

He started thinking about the first time he saw her. He had thought she was a student. He was taking a computer class for work. The boss had a bright idea about getting all the inventory, the records, on a computer, and since the other bartender would not touch a computer, Mike volunteered.

The class was fun in a way, and he was thinking maybe he'd take another one, something different. It was a community college. You could take things for no credit, it didn't cost much. He was getting a little restless at the bar.

He was wondering what to take, when he saw a very pretty student in the hallway. She was looking at the bulletin board, and Mike, who was not shy about pretty women (though he was about most things), stopped and asked, "You know of a good class to take?"

She looked directly at him, didn't seem to be afraid of him, although he scared some people. Tall, long-haired, tattooed, he looked more like a janitor than a student, and he knew it.

"I hear the American Short Story is good."

"You going to be there?"

"Yes."

Mike had walked off and signed up for the class. It was a day class, he worked nights, what the hell.

And when he walked in and saw she was the teacher, he had to laugh.

It was a good class. He read his first book ever for this class. *To Have and Have Not.* It was the first book he tried to read that seemed to have something to do with real life. He liked hearing what she had to say about the writers.

But best of all he liked watching the teacher. She was so pretty. She moved as graceful as a deer. She always wore long skirts and light sweaters. He liked to picture what she looked like underneath. . . .

Everyone got up to leave, and Mike realized class must be over. He gathered up his notebook and book.

"Michael," she said. "Could you see me after class for a minute?"

When she'd first called roll, she'd asked each person what they preferred to be called, which was nice. He'd said "Michael," though no one ever used it.

Now what? he thought. So far he hadn't made a good impression on her. Two weeks ago he forgot and wore his gun to class. When she spotted it under his jacket, she called him out into the hallway and gave him what-for.

"I have a permit." He still shouldn't wear it into a school building, he knew that.

"I don't care if you have a handwritten note from God Almighty. Get that thing out of here."

He had, and she made no objection when he slipped back into class.

Now he stood next to her desk, trying to think of what he could have done. Maybe his staring had bothered her.

She looked up at him, and paused, and seemed to change her mind.

"Would you mind not wearing your ball cap in class?" she asked. "It really makes it hard to see your face."

Mike took it off. It was so much a part of him he felt like she'd asked him to go half-naked.

"That's much better." She had dark blue eyes, the color the sky got ten minutes after sunset. "You have nice eyes."

He was startled at hearing her repeat what he had been thinking.

"Can I ask you something?" she said.

"Okay."

"I don't mind you always sitting in the back, but can you tell me . . . why you are always watching the class? When I bore people, they usually look out the window. You're always looking at the other pupils, watching for something. What is it?"

Mike, relieved she hadn't said anything about watching her, tried to think. Suddenly he laughed. He knew what she meant.

"I'm a bouncer in a bar," he said. "I have to watch for fights building up."

"You think the class is going to break into a fight?"

"Well, when Mrs. Greemore said Henry James was better than Twain, I thought Mr. Lewis was going to pop her one. Sorry. It's habit."

She laughed, too. "Well that solves that. Thanks for taking off your hat."

Mike nodded. She must have been looking his way a lot if that bothered her so much.

He didn't wear the hat the next day. He knew she could see him better, and tried to keep his eyes on his book. But sometimes he had to grin to himself. He could feel her watching him.

VISIT

"So how's it going?" Terry asked.

He looked different, but not as different as Mike had thought he would. Anyone would change in almost five years. Hair a little longer, messy. A tooth missing. New scar on his upper lip—just new to Mike though, you could see it had been there a while.

"Okay," Mike said. They didn't have to talk through a glass wall on a phone, just sat at small table. He could have hugged Terry if he felt like it, but he didn't.

"Mom says you're a bartender now."

"Yes."

"Kind of like putting a fox in a hen house ain't it?"

They were the same age, but Mike could see Terry now looked older than he did. Was older than he was.

"You still hitting the booze pretty hard?"

"Sometimes," Mike said. He was going to tonight, that was for sure. For a second he wished he had a bottle out in the truck.

"You can get it in here. You can get just about anything in here. Except a woman."

Mike couldn't think of anything to say to that.

"Mom told me you and Amber broke up."

"A long time ago. Not too long after. . . ." Amber, the one girl Mike had who thought she chose the right one—but she had loved Terry, too, loved him the way a guy wanted his girl to love his brother.

The old Terry, anyway, the happy-go-lucky one, who had always been able to talk his way out of anything.

"Sorry to hear it. She was a real nice girl."

"Yes," Mike said.

They sat quiet for a minute.

Mike had been a loner all his life, but this was the one person he could always talk to. They had been raised as brothers, were closer than twins, this face was once as familiar as his own reflection in a mirror. . . . Now the cousins sat silent.

"You're up for parole next year," Mike said finally.

"Yeah,"

"You want to move back in with me?"

"Mom wants me to stay with her for a while. We'll see how long that lasts."

No use thinking things would be the same as they used to be, Mike thought. But still. . . .

"I might be able to get you a job," Mike said. "We're havin' a hard time getting honest help in the bar."

Terry looked at him and gave a short, ugly laugh, nothing like the laugh he had before.

"So they'd hire a felon?"

Mike hadn't thought about that. But still, Terry was very honest, in his own way. No thief.

But as he looked at this man, this stranger, he knew there was no telling what Terry was these days. Who he'd become. What he might do.

God, Mike thought.

They'd shared everything from the beginning—family, blood, and history. Their moms were sisters, their dads brothers, they had the same sets of grandparents. You'd be hard put to find a baby picture of one without the other. They'd shared a playpen, a dog, a first duck hunt. Learned to water ski the same day. Helped each other figure out how to smoke. Terry had gone after it so hard he made himself sick. "Slow down," Mike had said. "We'll get it. . . ."

Shared the mind-numbing grief the day their dads were killed in a car accident. First drunk. First joint. Swapped notes on the first sex. Had the same friends, both the good and the bad. . . .

And they should be sharing this—but Mike was walking free.

"Thanks for looking after Mom," Terry said.

"You know I'd do that."

"Yeah. I knew you'd do that."

Quiet again.

"Sorry I have not been good at writing," Mike said awkwardly.

Terry's letters had scared him. Bitter funny, not funny like he used to be. Strange. Sometimes so weird Mike was sure he'd gone nuts.

"Don't worry. You were never big on words."

That was true. Terry could talk rings around anyone, Mike was shy—yet Mike had known Terry listened to him, needed him, to keep him grounded, steady, to supply the common sense. Then the one time that could have made a big difference, Mike shrugged and went along. . . .

The guard said "Time," and both stood up. Mike wondered if his cousin was as relieved as he was. Still, something he had wanted to say for almost five years was fighting to get out.

Mike looked down but said, "Man, I . . . I am so sorry. It was just a piece of goddamn luck. I should be in here with you. . . ."

Still, Mike thought, it's not like I really got off scot-free.

He felt a hand on his shoulder, and met Terry's eyes. The same ones he knew so well. . . .

"There's not a day goes by," Terry said, "that I don't thank God you are not in here with me."

Out in the parking lot, Mike took a deep breath. He'd had a fear, all these years, that if he ever went into that place, he'd never get out. But here he was. . . .

He'd been scared, too, that if he ever saw Terry in there, he'd start crying and not be able to stop. But he waited until he was in the truck for that.

THE SWEETEST SOUND

Mike wasn't sure what woke him up. Cat fight, maybe. The thunder was beginning to roll away, and Mike could sleep through thunder anyway.

Then he heard another sound, a cry or a moan, and he slipped out of bed and down the hall to his parents' room.

Everything seemed wrong, disturbing—the bedside lamp on low, his mom kneeling on the side of the bed, her arms around his dad's shoulders, his dad sitting on the edge of the bed, in his boxers and T-shirt, his head in his hands.

Mike had never been in that room at night, couldn't make any sense of the scene. Then his mom saw him, wiped at her eyes with her wrist, and said, "It's okay, honey. Your dad was having a bad dream."

The grown-ups didn't have bad dreams, everyone knew that. Mike was still confused.

Then his dad lifted his head and saw him, and Mike was more terrified than he'd ever been in all his nine years.

Not of his dad, Mike was never afraid of his father. But the fear, the despair, the helplessness he saw in those hollow dark eyes. . . .

Mike's dad could fix plumbing, change the oil in a car, filet a fish, gut a duck. He wasn't afraid of the drunks stumbling in and out of the bar next to the hardware store. He knew what to do when a tornado was coming. He could hold a steady job whether it bored him or not, while Uncle TJ was always running off to try something new. The one time he got a ticket for speeding, Mike could tell he wasn't afraid of the policeman.

"Michael?" The voice was hoarse, almost not recognizable.

His father held out his arms, and Michael went into them, was immediately pulled in between his dad's legs, gripped tightly. His dad buried his face in Mike's neck, sniffing hard. Mike shifted, a little uneasy; he'd taken a half-assed bath after playing ball with Terry, helping mow the lawn before the storm. He didn't think he could smell too good.

But his dad breathed in like he was trying to smell the blood in his body, like it would smell like wildflowers instead of grass and dried sweat. He was listening to Mike's heart intently, as if it would drown the pounding of his own.

As if it was the sweetest sound, the sweetest music.

Mike stood, knowing he was needed. But the sense of dread overwhelmed him. What did the grown-ups have to fear?

He knew when he was grown up, his own fears would be gone—like not being able to find his room first day of school, that maybe driving a car would be beyond him, that he might not be good enough for big-league baseball after all.

Maybe there was so much more out there than Mike realized. When he put his arms around his dad's neck and clung, he wanted reassuring, although he realized that was his own job right now.

"Sorry, Son." His dad slowly released him. "I know I must have scared you."

Mike didn't want to nod, so he said nothing.

"You go back to bed now. I'm fine."

Mike's dad twisted the chain on his neck, flipping the tags that hung from it.

"Go on, honey," Mom said. She was rubbing Dad's shoulders now. Mike went back to bed and fell asleep immediately. Nothing was mentioned the next day.

When Mike was a grown-up, when he could fix plumbing and filet a fish, and the only thing that scared him about the drunks around the hardware store was that he might end up just like them, he realized that changing the oil in his truck was no safeguard against anything except a burned-up engine. . . .

He knew what to do when a tornado was coming, but that knowledge was useless if there weren't any around. . . .

And that wasn't the kind of stuff he wished he could ask his dad about now, anyway.

Mike would never be wise like his father. He quit a job that paid good money, just because he didn't get along with his boss. He cursed at the cops who kept giving him tickets, instead of not driving too fast.

But maybe he learned something in the ten years he had with his dad.

Because for a short while, he too had someone to cling to, when the bad dreams got heavy. Had someone whose skin smelled like wildflowers. Whose heartbeat drowned the pounding of his own.

And it was the sweetest sound, the sweetest music.

HOMECOMING

Aunt Julie was cleaning up the mess in the front room when Mike came back in with the beers.

In the kitchen, the women were taking advantage of her absence, their shushing whispers revealing the topic of the conversation as clear as shouts.

Except for Uncle Hiram and his fat-assed Jr., rooting and snorting around the leftovers, most of the men had left, preferring to take their speculations to the tavern.

Mike helped Aunt Julie stuff paper plates and cups into the garbage bag. The "Welcome Home Terry" banner was hanging by one tack, and Mike yanked it down and stuffed it in the bag, too.

It had been like watching kids poke a bear with a stick.

"He looks good, don't he?" Aunt Julie said.

"He looks tired."

Mike had never seen Terry tired like this. Exhausted maybe, after a long day of water-skiing, a weekend of bar-hopping, but not . . . worn out. Faded.

"He'll be fine." Aunt Julie patted Mike's shoulder. "They didn't break him, honey. Terry's still here. Don't you worry about him."

There was a shocked titter from the kitchen, and Mike clenched his teeth.

Aunt Julie's face hardened for a moment. Then she said, "Family's good for two things. Bring you joy," she gave him a quick hug, "or teach you patience."

Patience. That was it. In all their twenty-nine years, Mike had never seen Terry patient before now.

Lazy, hell yeah. Terry could be damn lazy. He'd always let Aunt Julie wait on him hand and foot, and they both acted like he was doing her a favor. Mike couldn't count the times Terry had conned him into doing his chores, his homework.

But Terry never took bullshit from anyone.

Terry came in, dropping on the couch next to Mike, putting his boots up on the coffee table.

Mike handed him a beer. "I bet you could use this."

"No shit." Terry gulped half the beer down. "I didn't see all these people claiming to be related to me at the trial. And they sure weren't filling up the visitors' room on weekends."

Mike mumbled, "Uh . . . I . . ."

"I didn't mean you, bro."

"They're really pissin' me off. Half of 'em are acting like you're going to jump up and cut their throats."

"Can't say the thought didn't occur to me." Terry paused. "You know what they're all dyin' to ask me, don't you?"

Mike changed the subject. "I might be able to get you on at the bar."

"Don't think the parole board would go for it. This'll shock you, but you do associate with known felons in that place."

Mike laughed.

"Naw," Terry went on. "I'm going to hook up with LeRoy, go back to framin' houses. He owes me one. One of our best customers in the old days."

Darlene wandered into the room, a scrawny girl in her late teens sporting a big frizzy perm with the front curls ironed in place, the rest hanging down her back in a tangle. Mike remembered her as a little kid, finger either in her nose or in her mouth, sneaking around, trying to catch them drinking beer or smoking, so she could run tattling to the grown-ups.

Now she wagged her finger at Terry, shooing his feet off the coffee table. Terry removed his boots, straightened up a little. Darlene sat down on the table, leaning forward conspiratorially.

"I just want you to know, Cousin Terry, I was praying for you every day."

"I appreciate that, Darlene."

She glanced around. "You always were my favorite cousin."

Terry looked toward Mike and said, "Try to live with it, bro."

Darlene didn't seem to catch it. She was still leaning forward, an unhealthy excitement in her whisper.

"Can I ask you something? It won't go no further than me, I swear. When you were . . . in there . . ." she took a breath and went on, "did . . . did anyone ever . . . *do* you?"

The answering voice gave Mike chills: "Any *doin'* that got done, I did it."

Darlene's eyes popped.

Terry relaxed, gave her a friendly smile. "Seems like you woulda grown us some boobies by now, Darlene. You low on woman juice or somethin'?"

Darlene screwed her face into a persimmon. "Aunt Julie!" she hollered. "Terry's makin' fun of my titties!"

Aunt Julie hollered back, "Terrance James MacIntosh, you behave!"

"Yes ma'am," Terry called.

Darlene was still sniffling, staring at him accusingly.

"Tell you what, Darlene. I know something that could remedy that problem."

"You do?"

"Yep. Got it from a reliable source. You go get you a wad of toilet paper and come back in here."

He and Mike looked at each other as she left.

Darlene came back in with a thick fold.

"Now you take that and rub it right down there between them."

Darlene pulled her T-shirt down a little, reaching to rub vigorously between her small breasts.

"That's right," Terry said. "You just do that every morning and you'll see some big changes soon."

After a minute she said, "I still don't see how this will help anything."

"Worked for your butt, didn't it?"

A moment of silence, then Darlene's jaw dropped in horror. She fled the room, her wail of "Aunt Julie!" trailing after her.

Terry sighed contentedly, put his feet back up on the table. Mike hooked an elbow around his neck and pulled him over to kiss the top of his head.

They clinked their beers together.

NO WHITE LIGHT NO TUNNEL

Mike forgot to lock the front door before he started wiping tables.

It had been a busy night in the bar. He had pulled beers, poured shots, washed glasses, stopped three fights, listened to half a dozen sad stories. When the last customer left, surprisingly early for a busy night, it was not yet two.

He meant to turn off the flashing "Open" sign, too, but didn't. So when he heard the front door open behind him, he had only himself to blame.

"Sorry, man," he said. "We're closed."

He turned and saw the gun. Funny, how he concentrated on the guy's face, trying to remember details—knowing, sick, why he probably hadn't bothered to put on a mask. At the same time all he could see was the gun. It was a .38.

"The cash."

"Sure," Mike said. Ed had the cash in the back. He was wondering how to break that news when they both heard a noise from there.

Mike couldn't remember if he had made a move or not. The next thing he knew he was flat on his back. He felt like someone had slammed him in the chest with a tire iron. He had never been shot before but somehow didn't picture it feeling like this.

There was a scramble at the door—Ed jumping over him to chase the guy into the parking lot. Mike heard the boom of the bar's shotgun. He hadn't heard the first shot. It was like his mind skipped right over it.

Mike looked around. The bar looked different from this angle. Gum and God-knows-what stuck under the tables. Stains on the ceiling tiles.

For some reason he had it in his brain that he could ask for do-overs, go back fifteen minutes, get it right this time. It was starting to hurt now.

"Mike!" Ed ran back in, knelt beside him. Ed grabbed a bar towel off the table, yanked Mike's shirt open, pressed the towel against his chest. That hurt too, but Mike didn't say anything except, "You get him?"

"Yes. Stay down," Ed ordered. Mike was used to taking orders from the older man; he wasn't going to argue now. Then Ed jumped up, and Mike almost grabbed at him.

"Medics and cops," he heard Ed bark into the phone. He gave the bar address slowly, with a couple of simple directions and, "Medics and cops. You got that?"

Ed was beside him again, clasping his hand in a grip. It felt strong and warm.

"That was from 'Nam, wasn't it?"

"What?"

"Saying 'medics' instead of 'ambulance.'"

"I guess so," Ed answered.

Mike said, "My dad was in 'Nam."

"I know."

Mike's fingers were rubbing at the floor, like they were trying to get a grip on it, and it felt too sticky.

"The floor's wet," Mike said. "That's not beer, is it?"

"You're a pretty good drinker, kid, but you're not going to bleed beer."

"Ouch," Mike said. It hurt to laugh. He paused.

"He never told me anything about it. 'Nam I mean. He died when I was ten. Maybe he was just waiting till I got older."

"It's nothing you want your kids to know about."

After a minute, Mike said, "I don't see any white light. No tunnel."

"Just as long as you don't see any yawning red pit with imps you'll be fine."

"Man, if I had known it would make you be funny, I would have got shot a long time ago."

Mike was out of breath when he finished that sentence. Now it really hurt to breathe. It felt like there was an elephant standing on his chest.

"Hang in there, Michael."

"Thought my name was Dumbass Kid."

"Sometimes you act like it's your job description."

"My dad called me Michael."

"I know."

Mike was quiet for a minute. Then he said, "You think that bozo's crawling around the parking lot like a half-squashed bug?"

"We can hope. You want me to go check?"

"No! . . . no." Mike shifted around, trying to escape the pain. "Shit! Fuck this, man! It hurts."

"I know," Ed said.

God, Mike thought. God. . . . He remembered the last time he had been in a church. He must have been nine. In the middle of whatever the preacher was saying, Mike's dad got up, took Mike by the hand, and left the church.

He was going to write that story sometime, he'd thought, the way his dad had smoked one cigarette after another, pacing, while they waited for church to be over, for Mom to come out. How upset he had been.

"That's not God," Mike's dad said finally. "What that preacher was saying. God is not fire insurance. God would like to help people, Michael. It upsets Him to see how bad we screw ourselves up. People make their own hell. God doesn't send them there."

"Okay," Mike had answered, ashamed to admit he hadn't really been paying attention, just waiting for church to be over, thinking about getting home, playing ball.

His parents had had a fight about it, one of their rare ones, but his dad never went back to that church. And wouldn't let Mike go either.

He meant to write that story, except he couldn't think of an end. But now it helped, picturing God the way his dad had told him.

"He'd been in a war, maybe he found out something . . ." Mike said aloud. "You find out things in a war, don't you?"

"Yes."

Mike tried to sit up, but Ed gently shoved him back down. They could hear a siren now, in the distance.

"Damn," Mike said, "this is going to be one mother of a hospital bill."

"Work-related. You're covered."

Mike couldn't see Ed too well now, his vision was blurry. But he heard him ask, "Anything else you're scared of?"

"Hell, yeah," Mike gasped. "Lots of stuff."

He was terrified, things to be scared of lining up in his mind, waiting their turn. . . .

"I'll tell you something I learned. Pick one."

"What?"

Ed said, "Pick one thing to be scared of. But one thing you can handle if you concentrate."

Mike thought. The siren was closer now.

"I'm scared I'm going to yell, make some kind of noise when they come to move me. I don't want to."

"All right," Ed said. "You concentrate on that."

INTERVIEWS WITH S. E. HINTON

Conducted by Teresa Miller

"It was cliché, he knew. But he meant it classic."—Tim

My father's typewriter, which I learned to type on.—S.E.H.

THE OUTSIDERS

July 13, 2006—Tulsa, Oklahoma

I have visited with Susie Hinton in her home before, but this time is different. Susie is going on record about her career as one of America's most popular writers. It is an especially warm day, and before we formalize our conversation, we take a moment to admire the caladiums lining her front walk, some red and some white, their deep green veins accentuating the contrast. Inside, Susie's fifteen-year-old Australian shepherd, Aleasha, is asleep on the kitchen floor and doesn't budge as we make our way to the refrigerator. I'd noticed once before that Susie has the same Franciscan apple dishes my grandmother had left to me, and this afternoon she explains that they had belonged to her mother. The dishes, like her early stories, place us in the same generation, and

I note that for such an accomplished person, she seems very relaxed in ordinary circumstances. She offers me a glass of wine, a Beringer chardonnay, and we settle in her den to talk. The focal point of the room is an old Underwood typewriter mounted on a roll-top desk.

Even though The Outsiders *is true to the 1960s, when teenagers were known as "Socs" and "greasers," what is it about the book that makes it timeless?*

If you've got ten kids in a class, they're going to divide into the in group and the out group. I get so many letters from kids saying, "We don't call them 'Socs' and 'greasers'; we call them 'jocks' and 'punks'; we call them 'preps' and 'skaters.'" The names change, the uniforms change, but the groups go on forever, and kids instantly recognize that aspect of the book. Another thing is the emotional intensity. I wrote it when I was sixteen. When I read it as an adult, the emotions seem a little over the top, so I couldn't have written that book later. I wrote it at the right time in my life, because that was exactly what I was feeling, and that's exactly what the kids who read it today are feeling, too.

Most scholars agree that The Outsiders *created a whole new publishing genre, young adult literature. Was there anything missing from your own life that motivated you to write beyond traditional frameworks?*

One of the reasons why I wrote *The Outsiders* was that nothing realistic was being written for teenagers. If you were through with the animal books and you weren't ready for an adult book, there was nothing to read except *Mary Jane Goes to the Prom* and *Tommy Hits a Home Run.* I couldn't find anything that dealt with teenage life as I was seeing it, so in one sense I wrote it just to have something to read.

What sort of books did you read?

I was a very eclectic reader. I loved Shirley Jackson's *The Haunting of Hill House*. Naturally you can assume from reading *The Outsiders* that I had read *Gone with the Wind*. Actually when I re-read *The Outsiders*, I'm amazed by how literate Ponyboy is. He mentions reading *Great Expectations*.

Your father was dying while you worked on the book. Do you think that on some level you were trying to process your grief through the story you created?

Oh, absolutely. At the time I didn't make the connection. Now it's so obvious, looking back, that I was writing it to escape my own reality. There are a couple of deaths in *The Outsiders*, too, so I was dealing with death in my own way, but I write so much from the subconscious that it takes me years to figure out what a book's about.

Clearly you had an extraordinary gift as a writer, even at an early age. In what ways were you a typical teenager?

I wasn't really typical of the female culture at that time, because all girls got to do was rat their hair and outline their eyes in black. I didn't want a boyfriend with a hot car; I wanted my own car. I think about the actors who are in my movies. Off camera, they were just these goofy, normal prank-playing teenagers, but when the camera was on they were serious artists. And in a lot of ways I identified with them. When I got behind my typewriter, I was serious. Not that I took myself seriously; I took my writing seriously.

You told me a story about getting your first typewriter.

Oh! My first typewriter. I taught myself to type on my dad's old Underwood, and I still have it. I must have had fingers of steel to type on that thing. I'd been writing for a long time at that point; I started in grade school. When I was in the ninth grade I had my cocker spaniel bred, sold her puppies, and bought my first Underwood. It wasn't electric, but it was still easier to use than my dad's Underwood.

How did you fit writing into your overall life as a high school student?

Writing actually was my life as a high school student. I wasn't the kind of kid who had to be hanging out with people all the time. I had a boyfriend; we went out once a week. But I was very serious. I was not unhappy being alone. I'm still not unhappy being alone. I'm not scared of hearing a thought go through my brain—unlike people with cell phones glued to their ears. I have a great imagination, and I love using it.

Did you write regularly or just when ideas or stories came to you?

I wrote regularly, and I read a lot of cowboy stories, a lot of horse stories. I had this mythical cowboy town called Clearwater County. I even made up a newspaper for Clearwater. So I'd done a couple of other books by the time I wrote *The Outsiders.* The year I started *The Outsiders* I was absolutely immersed in it. I took it to school, wrote it on the dinner table. The first draft was about forty pages, single-spaced, but I kept writing more flashbacks, adding more detail.

Critics have noted how beautifully you structured the book. How important do you think the circular ending is to the overall story? We begin and end with Ponyboy.

I love that ending, and I wish I could say I originated it, but actually in the seventh or eighth grade, during my sci-fi period, I read a short story that did that same thing. I'm sure that's what gave me the idea.

Did your family members realize how dedicated you were to your writing?

No it was just like, "Oh, gosh, she's going to outgrow this sooner or later." My mother was upset I wasn't watching television with the rest of the family.

What about your friends?

My close friends knew that I wrote, but I was always kind of a loner. I was eccentric. I had friends in different groups, but I couldn't even conform to the nonconformists.

Was it hard to get a publisher to take you and your work seriously because you were so young?

Actually not. I've always had strange coincidences happening in my life. A friend of mine's mother read *The Outsiders*, sent it to an acquaintance of hers who was a professional writer, and got the name and address of her agent. The agent, Marilyn Marlow at Curtis Brown, Limited, in New York, called to say, "I think you've caught a certain spirit here, and I'm going to see what I can do with it." She sold the book to Viking Press, the second publisher that saw it. I got my contract on graduation day that spring and stayed with Marilyn as my agent for thirty years—until her death.

Is it true you almost got an F in your high school creative writing class?

The year I was writing *The Outsiders* I made a D in creative

Marylin E. Marlow
Curtis Brown Limited
575 Madison Ave
New York, N. Y.

Dear Miss Marlow:

Mrs. ~~Elizabeth Thompson of Tulsa~~ suggested that I write
~~you concerning my Book, A Different Sunset~~. I started this
book about three years ago as a short story, but I soon
found that I couldn't get all I wanted to say into a short
story. It was started for fun, but it means more to me than
that. There's a lot of social injustice in teen-age life,
and while I did research for this book I learned to understand, but not accept, some of it. I am now seventeen, but
I still feel the same way about my "greasers" as I did then—
that you can't judge a boy by his haircut and his clothes.
I only changed my opinion of the "socials" or "soc.s"—I
realize now that even the In-Crowd can have problems.
 You might like to know that quite a few people in the
book are from real life. The true-life counter-part of Two-
Bit Mathews, for instance, drove me to school yesterday. He
and his friends are my real inspiration. I mentioned that to
them one time, and they got a nice laugh out of it. They re-
fuse to take me seriously, and I'm glad of it. This way, they
let me in on things they do and think and feel. That's why
this book is important to me. Even if only a few people change
their conception of "greasers" and "soc.s" it will be worth
all the time I've put into it.
 I plan to go to Tulsa University for at least two years,
espiecally after hearing Mr. Weathers give a lecture. I am
interested in anything that can help me write better and understand more of what I read. (And I read anything I can get my
hands on.) I am sending you the third and final copy of my book.
I'd appreciate any criticism or suggestions you could give me.
Thank you for your time and trouble,

                    Yours truly,

                    Susie
                    Hinton

My first letter to my agent, Marilyn Marlow.—S.E.H.

writing. It's probably because I was so focused on the book that I wasn't doing my work. Also I found out that publishers don't count off for spelling.

Publishing contracts always trump grades. How did your family respond to the news that you had sold The Outsiders?

My mother never read *The Outsiders* until after it was published. At first she was shocked senseless. She was running around asking, "What are the neighbors going to think? What is the family going to think?" Then, when it started getting good reviews and making some money, she began saying, "Wasn't that a nice little book that Susie wrote?" My sister was actually the person who sent the book off to Marilyn, because in idle conversation one day with my mother, I said, "If I sell my book, can I get a car?" My mother replied, "Oh, yeah, you sell a book, you can get a car. Right." My sister overheard and really pushed me to get the book bundled up and in the mail. She walked around for years afterwards, going, "I sent the book off, I sent the book off," and I said, "Yeah, and you put the first dent in the car, too."

Did you have any notion at that point that this book would take off like it did?

No, I didn't. I thought kids would like it, but I never dreamed it would have the impact that it's had. I mean, it's sold over fourteen million copies. It's in use in most middle schools and high schools in America, and it's been translated into twenty-seven languages. I just got a fan letter from a kid in Greece. And older people, who read the book when they were young, now write to say, "You literally changed my life, the way I think about things." I feel scared and humbled, because I don't think of myself as somebody who can change lives or should be changing lives. I tell them it's the message, not the messenger. I feel different about *The Outsiders* than I do my other books. *The Outsiders* was meant to be written, and I got chosen to write it.

You'd grown up in Tulsa, Oklahoma, and suddenly you were on a national stage. Were you anxious at all when you planned your first trip to New York?

I'd never been out of Tulsa, except to go to Texas to visit my grandparents, so I was excited about the trip. My mother was wringing her hands, saying, "An eighteen-year-old cannot go to New York City alone." So she sent my fifteen-year-old sister to take care of me. I had a great time, but *The Outsiders* was not an overnight bestseller. My first royalty check was for twelve bucks. Even in those days twelve bucks didn't get you more than three tanks of gas, so I went on to college. I ran into my statistics teacher a few years ago, and she said she hoped I knew she had cut me a lot of slack. I said, "I know you did, and bless you!" I did everything but kneel at her feet. I also had some professors who graded me very fairly.

Were you still writing?

I developed a really bad case of writer's block, which lasted for over four years. For the first time, I was aware of the audience. When I was writing *The Outsiders*, it was for me; I wasn't thinking about getting published. I still envy those days. I've never written anything with the idea, "Oh kids will like this," but in the back of my head now I know that somebody's going to review me. Not all reviews of *The Outsiders* were favorable. I remember *Kirkus* absolutely hated the book and said, "You can believe a kid wrote it, but kids are never going to believe a thing it says." Well.

Famous last words.

Yeah, famous last words. Finally my boyfriend, David, who is now my husband, got annoyed with me for being so gloomy. I'd been writing all my life and couldn't use the typewriter to type a letter. He told me that if I didn't write two pages a day, he wouldn't take me out in the evening. That was the great motivation for my second novel. I wanted to go out, so I'd write the two pages. I was very careful about each sentence. I was reading a lot of really good writers in college, and I'd magnified everything that was wrong with *The Outsiders*. I told myself I was going to do the new book right. The book, which turned out to be *That Was Then, This Is Now*, required very little rewriting. Technically I think it's a better book than *The Outsiders*, but it doesn't have its emotional impact.

Your given name is Susan Eloise. How did you become S. E.?

My publishers asked me if they could just use my initials because of the subject matter. They thought if reviewers picked up *The Outsiders* and saw that a girl had written it, they would read it with bias. The initials sounded great to me. I liked having a public name and a private name. At first, reviewers would mention that a young man had written the book, but after a while I wasn't a secret. I was on television; I was on radio.

Earlier you talked about your focus on male characters in the book. I wonder if you might elaborate on that a little bit more. Why exclusively male characters?

I had two close cousins who were like brothers to me, and I ran around with them and their friends. I liked to play football. I liked to hunt ducks. I liked to go fishing. I just thought if I wrote that girls were doing these things, nobody would believe it. It's easier for me to write from a male point of view. I know I'm convincing because I get letters from guys to this day saying, "Mr. Hinton, I like your books." The only book I've written from a female point of view is *The Puppy Sister*, an elementary-age book told from the viewpoint of a female Australian shepherd puppy. I switched gender and species. Other than that, I usually stay with the male characters.

How closely did you identify with your narrator, Ponyboy Curtis, in The Outsiders?

Ponyboy Curtis is probably the closest I've ever come to putting myself in a book, even down to the physical description. He had my ideas; he had my personality. And he and I both liked sunsets. My mother would yell, "Why are you taking so long to get the garbage can back in the house?" It would be because I was standing outside watching the sun set.

Wasn't Different Sunsets *your original title for the book?*

It was, but I had a wonderful editor, Velma Varner, who thought that title would be too "soft" for the story. I agreed. *The Outsiders* encompasses so many different levels. I'm glad I changed it.

Is the novel based on any of your actual high school experiences?

When a friend of mine got beaten up on his way home from school one day, I began a short story about a kid who got beaten up on his way home from the movies. That turned out to be the beginning of *The Outsiders*, but I didn't base anybody in the book on real-life people.

One story has it that you researched the book and got a feel for greasers by carrying a knife. Fact or fiction?

Fiction, fiction, fiction. I did carry a knife, but it wasn't like I was researching a book. I thought it was cool. I didn't use it for anything. It did come out in the washing machine once, but I told my mother it was a letter opener.

Why do you think so many myths abound about you and your writing?

I have no idea. People have written saying they knew my college roommate; I didn't ever have a roommate in college. I've had offers from people who want to do a movie of my life, and the very thought makes my skin crawl. I'm a real private person. That's why I rarely have my picture in the newspapers. I don't like being recognized in public. It startles me when I'm wandering around in the grocery store, usually in sweat pants and without makeup, and someone yells, "S. E. Hinton!"

And I'm sure you get lots of fan letters.

It's the guilt trip of my life that I can't answer all my mail. I just can't. I live a very simple life. I don't have help; I'm not in a castle with a big staff. I'm trying to keep myself as domestic as possible because I don't want to get isolated from realities. I think that's very important to my work. I just hope people realize there's a difference between me and the books. I'm a mother. I'm a wife. I'm a good friend. I'm a pretty good horseback rider. I'm a reader. Anything left over from that goes into my books.

Who is Jimmy, the person to whom you dedicated The Outsiders?

Jimmy is my cousin. We were closer than a lot of brothers and sisters, and I was hanging out with his friends when I was writing *The Outsiders*.

How did Jimmy respond when he found out you dedicated the book to him?

He didn't say anything. That's Jimmy. He's a quiet person.

One of the book's outstanding achievements is the way you're able to depict your male characters, all close in age and circumstance, so distinctly. How did you avoid teenager stereotypes?

I'm a character writer. I know my characters' astrological signs; I know what they eat for breakfast. It doesn't matter whether those details show up in the books themselves. I have to become my narrators the way actors become their characters.

What astrological sign is Ponyboy?

Ponyboy has the same birthday as I do, July 22; he's a Cancer, on the cusp of Leo.

Your characters' names add to their uniqueness. Instead of "Tom" and "Mark," we have "Ponyboy" and "Soda." How did you decide on these nontraditional names?

I don't know where "Ponyboy" came from, but I did know a guy whose name was "Soda." And I think the name "Johnnycake" probably came from Johnny's last name, "Cade." Kids love those names. One of my readers saw the TV show *My Name Is Earl*, and a character mentioned hanging out "Ponyboy-style." If he'd said "Bill-style," nobody would have known what he was talking about.

After Ponyboy, which character in The Outsiders *is closest to your heart?*

Actually every character any writer writes is a part of her; writers are the filter. As much as I was Ponyboy, I was every one of the characters in that book.

Johnny's an especially moving character. Did you know when you started the book that he was going to die, or did you discover that in process?

I discovered that in process. To me that's the way the story happened. I didn't make Johnny die; he died. I didn't have a clear frame for *The Outsiders* when I started it. I just sat down and began writing. I'd get stuck, go to school, and say, "I'm writing a book. This is what's happened so far. What should happen next?" I was taking help whenever I could get it. I came across a Robert Frost poem, "Nothing Gold Can Stay," in an English class, thought it said what I wanted to say in *The Outsiders*, and so I wrote it into the book.

"Nothing Gold Can Stay" seemed to give the book a central theme. Is it true that some people actually think you, not Robert Frost, wrote the poem?

That is true, which is not the worst thing that can happen to a writer! Sometimes I go to speak to librarians or teachers, and they'll introduce me with that poem. I'll get up and say, "I hope everyone knows that was actually written by Robert Frost." But it is definitely very, very tied into the novel. Even in casual references to the book, people say, "Stay gold."

That's how you sign your books many times.

Yes, people ask for me to sign with "Stay gold" all the time.

A lot of fans ask Ralph Macchio to sign his autograph that way, too.

Why do you think that poem resonated so much with you and your readers?

Because it's about the loss of innocence and about how the idealist in you has to come up against the compromise of living in the real world.

Did you ever consider telling this story in any point of view other than first person?

No. I'm very comfortable with the first-person narrative, but I do have to have the resources emotionally to bring me into the character.

As Ponyboy, you write some wonderful lines. In the heart of the novel, Ponyboy looks at Johnny resting on the couch and says, "Maybe people are younger when they are asleep." Do you remember where you were literally and figuratively when that insight came to you?

I have to admit that I don't know where a lot of that came from.

Also Ponyboy avoids pat descriptions of the people he loves. He speaks of Soda's "finely drawn, sensitive face that somehow manages to be reckless and thoughtful at the same time." Were you seeing Soda through Ponyboy's eyes or was he seeing Soda through yours?

I was seeing Soda through Ponyboy's eyes. I mentioned somewhere that Ponyboy likes to draw, to draw and sketch. He even talks about how he liked to sketch Dallas because he could get him down in a few lines. He's thinking like an artist.

You mentioned earlier that your editor wanted you to change the title of the book. What sort of editing process did you go through with The Outsiders?

Velma didn't tell me what to write. She just told me how to deal with what I'd already written. *The Outsiders* is very much my book, but it's a better book because Velma gave me suggestions. She was specific. I've developed lifelong friendships with my other editors—Craig Virden, George Nicholson, Ron Buehl—and they became a great part of my writing life, but Velma was the one who opened up my eyes to the editing process.

As you look back at the book as a more mature writer, do you view the adult characters any differently?

All kids like to think that their little land is completely off the map for adults. I wasn't ready to do adult characters at that point, so I don't miss them. The kids don't miss them. The one adult character that pops up is the guy at the church who doesn't rescue the kids because he's too fat to get them down.

When the book was first published, critics commented on what they viewed as the religious symbolism in the story, but you insisted that that was just their notion. Do you still feel that way?

If you want to look for religious symbolism in the book, you will find it. About the third time I got somebody's dissertation on religious symbolism in *The Outsiders*, I re-read the book with that in mind and, by golly, it's there. But lo, I bring you tidings: I didn't do it consciously. So much of my writing is subconscious. I keep hoping to find a way to take a nap and wake up with a chapter done. Johnny Cade is a Jesus figure who dies saving people. He comes back from death with his message of brotherhood for Ponyboy, and he dies between two thieves, Dallas and Bob. I mean, he writes in the dust of a church, "Be back soon," and signs it "J. C." The book even opens and closes with the line, "When I stepped in the light from the darkness."

At one point, The Outsiders *was the second-best selling paperback for young adults in publishing history, topped only by* Charlotte's Web. *What's your opinion of* Charlotte's Web?

I love *Charlotte's Web. Charlotte's Web* and *The Outsiders* are both about the same things. They're about death; they're about friendship; they're about sacrifice; they're about resurrection.

What do you think of the recent young adult bestseller Harry Potter?

I haven't read *Harry Potter.* I never was into fantasy. I've seen a couple of the movies, and I've enjoyed them. My reading time is so precious to me that I want to read what I want to read. But any book that gets kids into reading is great.

Earlier you said that you felt you were destined to write The Outsiders—*it was meant to be. Could you speak a little more about the role you feel destiny played in the book?*

The Outsiders almost died on the vine because it was published initially as a mass-market paperback, a drugstore paperback. Dell was about ready to stop printing it but noticed it was starting to sell well in several places and did some research. Teachers had found that they could get nonreaders to read it, and they were ordering books for all their classes. Teachers are my heroes anyway, but I'll tell you, they're the best damn advertising a writer can have.

You talked about the hundreds of fan letters you've gotten, people telling you that The Outsiders *has changed their lives. How has it changed your life?*

Well of course it's changed my life drastically. I've had the luck and the leisure to be able to write and make a living out of it. Frankly I could live off *The Outsiders*, so it's given me a lot of freedom as a writer. I can write what I want to without worrying about the audience. And it's given me a lot of satisfaction to be part of something that has touched so many peoples' lives and hearts. I just had somebody on the radio ask me how it felt being known for my first book. I said, "From what I hear, it beats being not known at all."

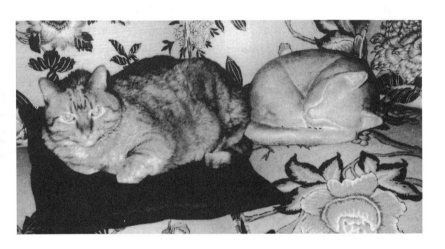

"He's okay, but I don't share the pillow."—Mr. Smithers

SEQUELS

Even though I've learned to expect the ceramic Siamese curled up in Susie's living room chair, it still startles me. The cat is territorial and seems to pounce on any imagination that bypasses it en route to the den, the room where Susie is most comfortable. Susie already has tumblers of wine waiting for us, and we assume the same places on the sofa that worked for us during our first interview. Ours is a relaxed conformity. We know where to plug in the tape recorder—there is an extension cord under the coffee table—but we also allow ourselves "unplugged" time in between questions to top off our glasses. Another Siamese stares at me from a portrait above the large-screen television. Like its ceramic counterpart, it flirts with the notion of being real. "That's Mr. Smithers," Susie says, but she is referring in-

stead to an actual cat that has joined us to sit rigidly atop the coffee table. Smitty, an orange tabby, looks porcelain. Susie claims as an aside that she keeps him because he matches her décor—the oranges and browns—but her affection is obvious as she explains he can disco dance on command. He isn't in the mood, so our thoughts grudgingly turn to fiction, real life, and some fuzzy distinctions.

So many wonderful things came to you courtesy of The Outsiders: *international recognition, financial security.*

I was making about two cents a book. I'll call it financial help in the first few years, but it certainly wasn't security.

During our last visit, you talked about the writer's block you developed after The Outsiders *when you were working on* That Was Then, This Is Now.

In the ending of *That Was Then, This Is Now,* when Bryon says he's emotionally drained from caring about people, he reflects my own state of mind. I was emotionally drained from having lived *The Outsiders* and then having it be over. It just wiped me out.

You've said what a help your boyfriend, David, now your husband, was to you while you were writing the book. Did that strengthen your relationship?

It's funny, because I got the contract on our wedding day. Before, when the contract for *The Outsiders* arrived on graduation day, I thought, *Graduation is nothing; I sold my book!* But when my contract came for *That Was Then, This Is Now,* I was thinking, *This is nothing; I'm getting married.*

Many writers—Harper Lee is an example—write such successful first novels, they wonder if they can ever write at that level again. Did you experience any of those feelings after The Outsiders?

I still think I can write something better than *The Outsiders*, but I've given up hope that I'll do anything that's as well loved. That doesn't bother me. How can you top something that has touched people the way *The Outsiders* has? I don't even worry about that.

Was there a defining moment for you when you realized that, because of your newfound celebrity, you were going to have to establish some boundaries for yourself and your fans?

At first I was as accommodating as I could be about giving speeches, but I've learned when to say no. I can be either a writer or a speaker. I hate speaking, love writing, so the choice is obvious.

You realized the story of The Outsiders *so completely that readers felt as if Ponyboy, Soda, and Darry were personal friends. How much pressure did you feel to write a sequel?*

I felt a lot of pressure to write a sequel. I still do feel a lot of pressure to write a sequel. If you go to fanfiction.net, there are more than two thousand Outsider stories, and a lot of them are sequels. I'm fine with fanfiction.net if that helps kids get the feel of writing, but to me *The Outsiders* stands where it is. I ended it at the right place. I'm not sixteen, no matter how well I remember being that age. I could not capture that moment again, and I don't want to capture that moment again. But I may write a sequel and put it in my safety-deposit box to be opened after my death, just to keep another writer from doing a sequel after the copyright expires. As much as I don't mind fanfiction.net, I'm uncomfortable with the thought of somebody else seriously messing with my characters.

Did the title of your second novel, That Was Then, This Is Now, *become a personal statement—as well as a great name for your new story?*

My subconscious works so well that, yes, it could be a personal statement, now that I look back on it. But at the time I wanted to use it as a metaphor for growing up and suddenly realizing you can't go on being a little kid. You've got to make some tough decisions. Sometimes they're not going to be the right decisions, but you've got to blunder your way through them.

When we first visited, you said that you feel That Was Then, This Is Now *is a better book technically than* The Outsiders. *Can you elaborate on what, in your opinion, makes it better technically?*

Because I had a little more control of my emotions; some of *The Outsiders* is over the top emotionally. You've got to control emotion with technique. Talent plus discipline equals art; you can't have one without the other.

In reviewing That Was Then, This Is Now, *the* New York Times *described it as mature, disciplined. What did you learn writing* The Outsiders *that made you more proficient when you were writing* That Was Then, This Is Now?

Going through revisions of *The Outsiders*, I learned not to be overly descriptive, but I'd been writing for many, many years and had been teaching myself the whole time.

You were enrolled at the University of Tulsa when you were working on That Was Then, This Is Now. *Did it seem strange to be sitting in a freshman comp class when you'd already made publishing history?*

It certainly didn't make it easier for me to get through

freshman comp; that was a hard class.

In what ways are Bryon and Mark, your lead characters in That Was Then, This Is Now, *different from Ponyboy and his extended family of friends?*

Oh, they're very different. I try not to repeat my characters at all. When I wrote about Mark, I kept thinking of him as a lion on Bryon's chain. And Bryon isn't Ponyboy in that he isn't as sensitive. He isn't aware of society until it knocks him in the head. He can't just sit and observe.

Did you ever find yourself slipping into Ponyboy's voice when you were writing as Bryon?

I'd left Ponyboy behind by that time, so I never had any trouble with Bryon's voice.

In That Was Then, This Is Now *you do allude to Ponyboy from time to time. He's become a local hero of sorts; your character Cathy wants to date him in the final chapters in the book. Did referencing him give you a sense of continuity as a writer?*

It did in that I wanted to mark the time and place for *That Was Then, This Is Now.* It happened a few years after *The Outsiders,* so I have Ponyboy do a walk-through. Also, Bryon, especially in the beginning, didn't like Ponyboy. He thought he was stuck up, thought he was vain because he was so good-looking. I wanted kids to see how easy it is to make wrong assumptions.

I mentioned how much I admired your edgy description in The Outsiders, *your ability to view your characters beyond stereotypes. In* That Was Then, This Is Now, *you demonstrate that same talent. When Bryon goes to visit Mark in the reformatory, he notes, "He had lost weight but somehow it had stretched his skin over his bones and slanted his eyes. He hadn't lost his looks but exchanged them." How distinctly do you see characters in your writer's eye?*

I usually see my characters very, very distinctly. Sometimes I even dream about them. When I do, they're not the actors; I see the characters. I guess that comes through, because usually people visualize my characters when they're reading them.

Why do you think some of your readers were frustrated with the way you ended That Was Then, This Is Now?

I've always said if you threw the book across the room at the end, you understood it. I wanted to show that there's not a happy ending for every story. In a lot of ways, growth is betrayal. Things change, no matter how much you'd like them to stay the same.

After the surprise success of The Outsiders, *did the publication of* That Was Then, This Is Now *seem anticlimatic?*

Maybe a little bit, but on the other hand it was certainly validation. The first book could have been called a fluke, but with the second, I could safely say I had a career.

Is it true that your third novel, Rumble Fish, *actually began as a short story?*

Yes, I wrote it for a creative writing class, but I knew it should be a novel. After David and I got married, we went to Europe and were hippies for a while. When we came back and moved to California so he could attend graduate school at Stanford, I started thinking about writing again and pulled out *Rumble Fish*. Plot is the hardest part of writing for me; I'm good with characters and dialogue. But with *Rumble Fish*, I already had the plot and finished it in about four months.

Didn't you originally write it from the viewpoint of Steve, Rusty-James's friend?

Yes, and I couldn't stand it. Steve is a very observant, articulate, smart kid. Like Bryon and Ponyboy, he could see a lot; he could say a lot. But I'd done that before. So I rewrote the story from the viewpoint of Rusty-James, who is not observant, not intelligent, and yet he still has to convey the identity of the Motorcycle Boy, who is so complex. I'd write a sentence and be proud of it as a writer, look at it again, think Rusty-James could not say that, and cross it out. As a writer, I'm most proud of *Rumble Fish*, because it's very straightforward; there's no foreshadowing.

You've commented in the past that Motorcycle Boy kept haunting you, goading you to tell his story. Did you ever consider telling it from his point of view?

I haven't got any more clue to what that guy's mind was like than anybody else does. He's an enigma to me. I couldn't tell the story from his point of view. He's way smarter than I've ever been. I was involved in mythology when I wrote this book, and the Motorcycle Boy was doing his community a service by becoming a local myth. At one point he says to Rusty-James, "I'm tired of being the Pied Piper for these people. I can't lead them. I don't know anywhere to go." When he does finally commit suicide by releasing the fish and liberating the pet store, so to speak, he knows he's creating a bigger myth than if he'd just gotten killed in a rumble.

I've heard that you first got the idea for Motorcycle Boy from a magazine photo.

That's true. I was flipping through a magazine, cut out a picture of this guy with his motorcycle, and then put it away with the idea of writing a story one day. Years later, when I was getting ready to write the book, I looked at the picture again and saw that I had cut it so close to the edge that I couldn't make out the name of the magazine. After *Rumble Fish* was published and I was on a publicity tour for my next book, *Tex*, I was in Washington, D.C., to appear on a television panel with some high school kids. While I was waiting for them in the studio, their teacher walked up to me and pulled out the same magazine photograph. I almost fainted. I had never mentioned the photo to anyone. The teacher explained that he'd thought it was an interesting photograph, had cut it out, then made the connection when he read *Rumble Fish*. He'd left wider borders, and I could see it came from *Saturday Review*.

You've had so many interesting synchronicities in your life. Did Rumble Fish *become representative of your own changing philosophical views? You'd been raised in the conservative Christian tradition, then suddenly became exposed to differing views through higher education and travel.*

Early on I rejected organized religion. As a child, I went to a very fundamentalist church and saw a man preaching hellfire and brimstone under a sign that said "God is Love." It turned me against organized religion for the rest of my life. It did not turn me against God. To me, organized religion is like organized social classes, based on exclusion. God is inclusive.

You've described Rumble Fish *as very stylistic and set in a vague way. Were you concerned at all about how the book would be received? In* Rumble Fish, *there are no allusions to Ponyboy and your anchor characters; it stands on its own.*

Because I was thinking mythically, I wanted the book set in

as vague a time and place as possible. When Rusty-James is recalling the good old days with gangs, he might as well have been thinking about when there were knights at the round table. Francis Coppola, who directed the movie version, understood this and told his actors that the story was set two years in the future.

How did the last two pages of Rumble Fish *reinforce the overall point you wanted to make with the novel?*

All through the book Rusty-James is saying, "I'm just going to be like the Motorcycle Boy." By the end of the book, he's staring at a body of water; he goes deaf for a minute; he's not seeing; he's not feeling. He has become the Motorcycle Boy, but it's not what he thought it would be. My point: do not identify with something you don't define, because you may be getting it all wrong.

After Rumble Fish *was published, one critic declared you a brilliant novelist. What was your husband's reaction? He'd been your primary reader for the book.*

David's the only one I let read works in progress—usually. He's a mathematician and doesn't really like to read. I'm a writer and don't like to add. But I can always count on David to say, "That's nice, honey," when I show him my stories. After the critics liked *Rumble Fish*, he said, "Aren't you kind of surprised that *Rumble Fish* is getting such good reviews?" And I'm like, well, no.

All of your young adult novels seem to stand out for you in different ways. What makes Tex *your personal overall favorite?*

I just loved being that character. I began writing *Tex* when I was still working on the galleys for *Rumble Fish*. By the time I was finished with Rusty-James, I felt like I'd been pounding my head against a wall—a stone wall—and I wanted to be somebody happy for a change. And Tex and his brother and his friends were all characters I had actually used in grade school or middle school for a completely different story and setting. It took me over three and a half years to write. I'd get busy and then realize I'd gone sixty pages off on a tangent. I'd put the book in the drawer for a long time, then pull it out and start writing again. It's the only one of my young adult novels I have ever thought I might like to write a sequel to, maybe using one of the Collins kids as a narrator.

You've described Tex as the least tough of your characters. Why is he still so admirable?

He's the least tough, but he's the strongest. He's not going to let things break him. I think of Tex as the counterpoint to *That Was Then, This Is Now*. Tex learned a bad truth about his family, and it could have turned him against his brother forever, but he didn't let it.

Mark, your troubled character from That Was Then, This Is Now, *reappears in* Tex. *What unfinished business did you as a writer need to take care of with him?*

I really believe that, even though I didn't realize it at the time, I was writing a different version of *That Was Then, This Is Now*, showing another road not taken. Something made me put Mark in as the hitchhiker in the story; it's done very subtly. Even though Tex and Mark are half-brothers, they live in separate worlds.

All your novels seem to revise our conventional definitions of family. How does Tex's encounter with Mark help you build on that theme?

Mark and Tex are very much alike—so much so that Tex even says the hitchhiker reminds him of somebody, but he can't think who. They came from different backgrounds but had the same genetic material. There was just something about Tex, though, that was stronger—maybe not so self-indulgent. Mark showed no regret for the way his own immediate family had been lost, whereas it devastated Tex to learn that the man he thought was his father really wasn't. But he learned to forgive and accept much more than his brother, who actually was Pop's biological son.

Critics have pointed out that Jamie in Tex *is one of your most fully developed female characters. Did you consciously work on building her persona, or did she evolve naturally?*

Naturally. I think girls who have a lot of older brothers are, most of the time, pretty spunky. They've got to hold their own, and Jamie was making the point that she had a lot more common sense than the guys, so it wasn't fair that she couldn't have a motorcycle, too. I felt the same way.

You set Tex *in a fictional suburb outside of Tulsa rather than in the city itself. Did that provide you with some flexibility?*

I spent a lot time in the country when I was a kid—my grandmother had a farm out in Nowata, and I loved being on that farm. When I was writing *Tex*, I was living in Bixby, and to a certain degree, it's a suburb. In small towns there's a difference. Not that the kids don't get into their little groups, but economically everybody's about the same. So the Collins family is an anomaly in *Tex*.

How closely does Tex's devotion to his horse parallel your feelings for your own animals?

Negrito in *Tex* is based on my horse Toyota. I raised him

from a colt and broke him to the saddle. I was always one of those horse-crazy little girls, but I had to wait until I was an adult to buy a horse of my own. I was twenty at the time and spent the last seventy-five bucks I had in the bank to buy this four-month-old colt. He still needed milk supplements. When we moved to California, I took him with me and put him with a regular trainer. He turned out to be a champion jumper. I just let him decide what he wanted to do. He died at twenty-three, and I was right there holding his head.

Are horses still as much a part of your life as they were back then?

Not quite as much, because I don't have the time or the energy. After twenty-five years of showing and riding around the ring, I bought myself a little trail horse.

Not only have you loved horses, you became an accomplished jumper. What makes the sport worth the risk to you?

I like an adrenaline rush. I like challenges. Even as a kid I was braver than I should have been. When I was going to New York to do the publicity for *The Outsiders*, I'd never been on a jet, but I wasn't scared. Any time you try to start a new book, it's damn scary. But there's something about me that likes to push that button in me that's scared.

You've described your fifth young adult novel, Taming the Star Runner, *as a horse story and a love story. Would you agree with novelist Jane Smiley, herself a horse lover, that all horse stories are love stories?*

There's something special about girls and horses, because horses are so big and so powerful, yet they'll befriend you. They want to know what you want them to do.

You discovered you were pregnant right after you started Taming the Star Runner. *What did that do to your writing schedule?*

I wrote my editors, told them I wouldn't be able to do the book for a while, and asked if they wanted their money back. But they told me just to write the book whenever I felt like it, so I mentally retired with my box of chocolate-covered peanuts and a book of baby names, never giving the novel another thought until Nick was about four. I enrolled him in a preschool, where he went three days a week from nine to two, and I rented an office on the same block. I still had my outline for the book, and the characters were in my head. I identified a lot with Travis, because he was a writer, and we'd had some of the same experiences. He sold his first book when he was sixteen, and there's nobody at home to tell but the cat. People think it's autobiographical, but it's not really. Travis seems especially self-centered.

He's trying to figure out who he is. That's the way you are at that age. He's a good-looking kid; he knows it and is constantly checking in the mirror, but by the last page of the book he's looking out the window at other people. So he's maturing. Basically I think *Taming the Star Runner* is about an artist trying to learn discipline. Travis watches Casey, who's very talented. She understands the importance of discipline as she works to transform a horse into a wonderful piece of art. By the end of the book, Travis realizes what they've got in common—he's sitting at his typewriter waiting for his next book, and she's waiting for the artistic challenge of her next horse.

Did you realize as you wrote Taming the Star Runner *that it would be your last young adult novel for a while?*

I didn't. I was so identified with the genre, I didn't even think about that at the time.

Unlike your other early novels, Taming the Star Runner *is in third person. Do you think you might have been subconsciously distancing yourself a little bit?*

When I'm writing a first-person narration, I really have to become my narrator, and I have to be totally involved with that narrator. My son was only four years old at the time, and I was emotionally involved with him. I didn't have anything to spare to become Travis at that point. But I did think I could write a book about Travis. As a writer, I wanted to prove to myself that I hadn't lost it. It had been eight or nine years since I'd written *Tex.* But in that time, I had worked on the movies, and I'd had my child and worked on him.

And the book's dedicated to Nick.

Actually it was supposed to be dedicated to Nick and David. David's been in all my dedications since *That Was Then, This Is Now,* but the editor left out the comma between "Nicholas" and "David." "Nicholas David" is Nick's full name, so for lack of a comma, a dedication was lost.

As you think through all your young adult novels, do you see a character–writer progression? For example, did you need to write as Ponyboy in The Outsiders *before you could ultimately write about Travis in* Taming the Star Runner?

Definitely. Ponyboy is so much like me. But as you get older, you appreciate other qualities in people or hidden qualities in yourself. Travis is very different from me, and he's certainly different from me as a teenager, though some of his thoughts on writing and some of his experiences in getting his book published were very similar to mine. As a mature writer, you realize there are other people/characters in the world besides you.

Where do you think Ponyboy, your alter ego, would be today?

Ponyboy would be writing mystery novels under the name of P. M. Curtis.

Hollywood meets Tulsa. —S.E.H.

MOVIES

JULY 20, 2006—TULSA, OKLAHOMA

It is already 105 degrees by the time I get to Susie's, and she is waiting at the front door for me so I don't have to ring the doorbell. Hers is a quiet life—no unnecessary doorbells ringing, no music playing in the background, no television voices emanating from back bedrooms. Before we start taping, she explains that she prepares for heat waves the same way she prepares for snowstorms, stocking up on everything she might need so she won't have to leave the house. Extremes, I suspect, have become her discipline, and as she sits barefoot on her favorite couch, her only concern is that readers understand that she is not Cherry Valance, that she is not a Soc. As if on cue, we're interrupted by a double whistle. "That's the two o'clock bird," Susie explains, acknowledging a clock her son has given her. "There's a different bird call every hour, but I only know the birds by their times, not their species." We also listen as Aleasha sighs in the background and as the day's mail takes its own time sifting through the window slot. Otherwise, the house pretty much stays on low volume and even routine conversations resonate.

Like you, Ponyboy Curtis in The Outsiders *loves movies. What extended role did movies play in your life when you were growing up in Tulsa?*

As a kid I was just interested in seeing a good story. I can't tell you how many times I watched *Old Yeller*. The first movie I ever saw in my life was *Peter Pan*. I was five, and my mind went berserk with all those images, all that story. I developed a huge crush on red-headed boys all through grade school. I used to think of myself as a movie buff, but later in life I met movie buffs, and I lag way behind. But I've always been interested in movies as a form of storytelling.

What were some of your other favorite movies when you were a teenager, Ponyboy's age?

I liked *Lawrence of Arabia*, but I was a little older than Ponyboy when I saw that. And *Bye Bye Birdie*—I thought it was great. Then, of course Disney movies, especially the documentaries on animal life. In my twenties I had a couple of traumatic movie experiences, one with *The Godfather*. Little did I know that Mr. Coppola and I would have a relationship one day. But I got so involved with the movie that, when it got violent, I came out of it shaking. And very shortly afterward, I saw *In Cold Blood*. I had read the book but didn't expect the flashback to the actual murders. I was so traumatized I quit seeing movies for a couple of years. I've always liked sci-fi; Bruce Dern's movie *Silent Running* is still one of my all-time favorites. I also like good scary movies—*The Haunting, The Others*.

When I was younger I was more intrigued with movie stars than movies; I have the feeling it was just the opposite for you.

When I was in grade school, I was totally entranced with Little Joe Cartwright. I couldn't have cared less who Michael Landon was, but Little Joe Cartwright was such a hottie. As I grew older, I wasn't the kind to form actor crushes, but I really like actors. I've found that they talk like writers, except there's absolutely no sense of competition, so you can have a good conversation with them.

Ponyboy "loned" it at the movies, because he felt that going to the movies with friends was like having someone read over your shoulder. Do you ever "lone" it at the movies?

Occasionally. I did with *Brokeback Mountain*. I ran out of people to see it with but wasn't through seeing it myself. I was going to see it once a week for a long time.

When you were writing your early novels did you see them as movies in your mind's eye?

I just saw them as books. I wasn't even sure, especially with *The Outsiders*, that I wanted them to be movies.

Why do you think Tex *was the first of your books to make it to the big screen?*

My fans helped me with *Tex*. Tim Hunter, who later directed *Tex*, had done a screenplay called *Over the Edge*, and he told me later that whenever he asked kids on the set what they read, they said S. E. Hinton. Matt Dillon, who was one of the actors in *Over the Edge*, even said, "Like, man, if you ever do get an S. E. Hinton movie going, I want to be in it." Disney was going into PG movies and called me. At first I didn't want Disney to do the movie—I mean, *Tex Meets the Seven Dwarfs*. The next thing I knew, an executive from Disney was on my doorstep wanting to go to lunch.

On your doorstep in Tulsa?

On my doorstep in Tulsa! We went to lunch, and he offered me the standard amount for a young adult film; I told him the money was okay. He asked if I'd like an expense-paid trip to Disneyland, and I said sure, I loved Disneyland. But I was still just staring at him, and he finally asked what else it was that I wanted. I said, "I've got a horse that's perfect for the horse part." My horse got the role, and Disney got the book. Toyota played Tex's horse in the movie and did a wonderful job. He loved the movie-making process. He just knew all of those cameras and lights were for him. And he adored Matt Dillon, Tex. Matt came in early, and I gave him riding lessons for a couple of weeks. I also taught Matt to always have carrots in his pocket. There's a scene in the movie where Toyota is nuzzling Matt's pockets, looking for his carrots.

A lot of writers aren't even allowed on the sets of their films. How involved were you with Tex?

The director, Tim Hunter, came to Tulsa and asked if I wanted help scout locations. I drove him to the Camelot Inn, across the street from where Tex tried to make a phone call after being shot by a drug dealer. And I drove him out to Bixby, where I lived, and showed him the area. Scouting locations is so funny. You just drive around until you see something you like, walk up to the door, and say, "We'd like to put your house in our movie." It's amazing. People always say, "Yes, take the house! You like the dog, take the dog; you like the kid, take the kid!" Then he had me help on wardrobe; he let me in on everything. One day when he was shooting a scene from a big, high angle, there wasn't room for anybody but essential crew on the platform, but Tim got me on, and I got to watch that shot.

You said in a previous interview that Tex *is your favorite of your young adult novels. Was it hard, even though you liked Tim Hunter, to turn your story over to him?*

After I talked to Tim, I wasn't afraid of him, but after my first meeting with Matt, I was scared to death of him. Tim had told me: "I've got this kid. He's going to be big, and he wants to do *Tex*." So, I'm in New York, imagining Little Bixby Cowboy, when up walks this street punk, who says, "Hey, S. E., I thought you was a man!" And I thought, *Oh, dear! I hope this kid's a good actor, 'cause he can't play himself.* Matt later told me one of the hardest things for an actor to do is to act innocent when he isn't. I still think Tex is one of his best performances.

How did you come to make your acting debut in the film?

Tim asked if I'd do a cameo. After weeks of watching other actors, I thought it looked easy, so finally I said okay. He cast me as the typing teacher, and at first I got nervous, but it worked great. The typing teacher is supposed to be a wreck; the kids had put caps on the typewriter keys. I ran in, hit my marks, and said my lines without even glancing down—did it in a couple of takes.

What was it like seeing Tex *in the theater for the first time?*

It was great, especially since it opens with a long montage—Matt riding Toyota. Anytime I think of Toyota now, I can get out the DVD and see him in his prime.

Did Toyota develop a star complex at all?

He had a big ego to begin with—he was a champion jumper—but for months after the movie I couldn't get him to move without yelling "Action!"

What sort of synchronicity brought Francis Ford Coppola into your life?

A group of kids in California wrote Francis a letter, telling him *The Outsiders* was their favorite book and asking him to please make it into a movie. Francis was intrigued—he really does love kids—and had his producer get in touch with me. For years I'd had people calling me, saying they were interested in doing *The Outsiders*, but I was afraid it was going to end up being *Ponyboy Meets Beach Blanket Bingo*. So I was reluctant to hand over *The Outsiders* to anyone until I realized I was talking to Francis Coppola's studio. Just a couple months before, I'd seen *The Black Stallion*, and had thought that if that movie had been based on one of my books, I would have been thrilled.

Since you were such a fan of Coppola's work, were you nervous at all about meeting him?

Francis was holding huge casting calls all over the country, one in downtown Tulsa, and I went to the auditorium. I was nervous about meeting him, and as I walked down the aisle, I realized he was kind of nervous about meeting me. So I walked up, shook his hand, and told him, "Mr. Coppola, I do have a problem with your doing *The Outsiders*. *The Godfather* is better than the book, and *The Black Stallion* is better than the book. Are you going to do that to me?" He laughed—and relaxed. So did I. After I drove him around some Tulsa neighborhoods, he decided he wanted to shoot on location. He asked me to help with the script and with the wardrobe. I was going, "Yeah, I can do this; I'm experienced."

How well did you and Coppola work together when you actually started developing the screenplay? To borrow Ponyboy's phrase again, you'd pretty much "loned" it as a writer.

Francis took a copy of the book, outlined the introspection in one color, the action in one color, the dialogue in one color. Then he cut it up and literally pasted it on sheets in the form of a screenplay and had someone type it up that way. By the time he handed it to me, it was the size of a phone book, and he asked if I minded cutting it for him. I hadn't done any writing on the script for *Tex,* except once in a while, when Tim would say he needed transition lines. But I'd learned a lot about movies from watching what Tim did with the script. He always said you cannot have actors saying more than three sentences or it sounds like they're giving the preamble to the Constitution. So I was interested in keeping *The Outsiders* moving.

You were in your thirties when you were working on the screenplay. How did it feel coming back to your story as an older writer?

I had learned to accept a lot of the book, partially because of the response to it. But I couldn't help coming up with better lines and dialogue. Francis had no problems with anything I cut, but if I changed a line, he'd ask if that was how it had been in the book. And I'd say, "No, but it's better." Then he'd remind me that we were making the movie for the readers and needed to keep it like it was.

Many of the film stars—Matt Dillon, Patrick Swayze, Emilio Estevez, Tom Cruise, Diane Lane—went on the become show-business superstars. Did you see that potential in them as you watched them on the set?

I don't know what virtue there is in being able to see talent in front of your face, but it was obvious that they were going to be great. I actually got Francis to ask Matt to read for Dallas, because I thought he would be perfect for the part. After Matt's first reading, Francis told him to go home, and

Matt thought he'd blown it. He didn't find out until later that Francis was saying, "You've nailed it; go home!"

You'd also worked with Emilio Estevez before, on Tex.

Emilio was very professional, but he was so good at improv. The whole scene in *The Outsiders* where he looks like he's going to help Ponyboy clear the table but takes the chocolate cake and a beer and sits down in front of the TV—that was total Emilio. Another time when Two-Bit, Johnny, and Ponyboy were walking home from the movies, a hat blew by, and Emilio grabbed it and put it on. It had blown off the head of a cameraman. Emilio just used it as an opportunity.

You mentioned how closely you collaborated with Matt on Tex. *How closely did you work with the actors on* The Outsiders *to give them new insight into the characters?*

I worked with the actors quite a bit. They were turned loose here in Tulsa with no adult supervision, and I immediately took it upon myself to be their mother. Rob Lowe even called me "Mom" half the time. I'd run lines with the boys. They were really sweet kids. I tried not to go to the hotel where they were staying very often, because I knew, even as a mother, there would be only so much that I could do, and I really didn't want to know what was going on. The night the Socs were drowning Ponyboy in the movie, the other cast members, in a show of camaraderie, were pretending to drown each other in the hotel fountain. A few years later, I went back to the hotel and the fountain was gone. I think I know why.

C. Thomas Howell played Ponyboy, the character you say is most like you.

Yes, and he had the flu—bad—the night we were drowning him in the fountain. It was in the upper thirties. We did have heaters around, but by the time you were dragged out of that fountain and put in front of a heater, you could get pretty cold. Tommy toughed it out, though. Nobody whined.

Have you stayed in touch with the cast?

I've stayed in contact with Matt more than the others. He lives in New York, and I visit the city a lot. As for the rest of us, we can go years without getting together, but when we do, we pick up where we left off, so that's nice. Emilio and I e-mail once in a very great while. Tommy Howell and Ralph Macchio came back to Tulsa in 2006 for the premier of *The Outsiders: The Complete Novel*, the new DVD edition of the movie. And that was so much fun. They hadn't changed a bit. Between interviews we took the limo that was at our disposal and visited our old haunts where we'd shot the film—the park, the Curtis house. Johnny's house had a pig on the porch, which was kind of startling. The same man who lived in the Curtis brothers' house during the shoot is still living there. He came out on the porch and talked to us. He said people from all over the world come to take pictures of that house.

How important was it to you for the movie to be shot in Tulsa?

It was great for me, because I got to go home at the end of the day instead of having to head back to a hotel. And the movie really looks like Tulsa, not L.A. One night when I was fourteen, a girlfriend and I were watching a movie at the Admiral Twin Drive-In and saw some "hoodie" guys trying to pick up these Soc girls. A few years later, I wrote that incident into the *The Outsiders*. When Francis came into town, the Admiral Twin was one of the first places I showed him.

Didn't you once drive past the Admiral Twin Drive-In at Tulsa and catch a glimpse of your Outsiders characters at the drive-in themselves, watching a movie within a movie?

Many years later, as I was driving home from the airport, I looked over toward the Admiral Twin and saw the drive-in scene from *The Outsiders* playing on the screen. It was like looking into mirror, into mirror, into mirror—way back to that time when I was fourteen.

Your talent brought all of this wonderful artistry to your hometown, but after the films were over, your new colleagues moved on to other projects, other cities. Have you ever considered relocating?

No, I've never considered relocating. In fact, halfway through *The Outsiders*, Francis said we worked well together, and he liked Tulsa, did I have anything else we could shoot while he was in town? I told him I had this weird book, *Rumble Fish*, but nobody got it. One day he walked in, waving the book, going, "I love this book—it's so weird; we'll make it weirder. We'll shoot it in black and white; the fish will be in color. And we've already got a cast here." During the shooting of *Tex*, Matt had told me that *Rumble Fish* was his favorite of my books, one of his dream roles, and if he wasn't too old when it got off the ground, he wanted to play Motorcycle Boy. He said if he was really old—like twenty-seven—he'd direct.

You actually wrote the script for Rumble Fish *while you were finishing up* The Outsiders?

Yes, we were still shooting *The Outsiders*, sometimes putting in sixteen- to eighteen-hour days. Francis and I wrote

Rumble Fish on Sundays, and we got the first draft done in two weekends. *Tex* was coming out. So at one point in my life, I was shooting a movie, advertising a movie, writing a movie. But *Rumble Fish* was not a fun shoot. It was hot, and we shot all of it at night. I'd made a vow that I was not going to get close to any of the actors on the new shoot. Except, of course, Matt. I just wanted to stick with my screenwriting job at that point, and I did. *Rumble Fish* is Francis's movie. He did everything else.

You yourself have said that Rumble Fish *was a different sort of story. Were you concerned at all in the early stages about how it would translate to the screen?*

I wasn't concerned, because Francis was one of the few people I've ever talked to who understood the book. It was about myth-making. The movie's much more visual, much stronger than the book, actually. It was an amazing experience for me as a writer to see Francis's interpretation, because it was just what I was thinking.

After your first movie appearance in Tex, *you also had cameo roles in* The Outsiders *and* Rumble Fish. *What parts did you play?*

In *The Outsiders*, I played the nurse in Dallas's room, which was so easy, because I was so used to being hassled by Matt at that point. I was really kind of proud of myself, because I had to walk in, hit my marks, say my lines, set props down, and bump into Emilio and Tommy, who were coming to visit Matt's character.

What about your role in Rumble Fish?

I played a hooker. When Francis asked me, I didn't think about the fact that we'd be working with the same crew from *The Outsiders*. There were thirty guys on the set and two women, and I was sitting around in that hooker outfit for days, because we'd get behind on the shooting. That was not fun, though it's funny now that I look back at it. In the scene, I end up grabbing Vincent Spano, who played Steve, and start unbuttoning his shirt. Did I do that? Oh, my God! When I watch all these movies now, they're more like home movies. I'm thinking, that's the day we were all sunburned, or that was the day I made Tom Cruise throw up because he ate too much.

Were you uneasy at all about being directed by Coppola? That put your relationship on a whole different footing; after all, he'd directed Pacino, Brando, the all-time greats.

Francis was always really sweet to me. I've kept my SAG [Screen Actors Guild] card all these years in case he ever calls again. I'm ready.

Do you believe that working so closely with Coppola in the films also made you a better novelist?

It certainly gave me a different take on my writing. I started thinking in terms of scenes.

Earlier you spoke of the new 2006 DVD release of The Outsiders, *subtitled* The Complete Novel. *Is the movie even better now?*

I think so, because we shot the whole book. Francis was very adamant about that, but there was a lot of studio pressure before it was first released, and he cut the heck out of it. I was shocked the first time I saw it in the theater. So much of it was missing. I didn't say anything; I'm not a movie director or a movie editor. But it was chopped up into one action, one action, one action. Francis—it turns out—started getting the same letters I was getting, wondering why favorite parts of the book had been left out. Finally, he replaced twenty minutes of deleted footage. Francis is the only director I've ever heard of who went back and re-cut a movie because fans of the book asked him to.

He also added a lot of period music to the soundtrack.

I think Francis was right to add the music. The original music was a little too grandiose for the story. I'm not very musically oriented, but I like Stevie Wonder's "Stay Gold" very much. And the music for *Tex* fits the rockabilly nature of that movie. I loved the soundtrack for *Rumble Fish*. Very startling at the time, and I've noticed that it really has influenced other soundtracks since then.

Your friend Emilio Estevez wrote the screenplay for That Was Then, This Is Now *and starred in the film. Why do you think it hasn't received the same level of recognition as* The Outsiders, Tex, *and* Rumble Fish?

People wondered why I was letting a twenty-year-old kid write the screenplay, but I was the same age when I wrote the book. Emilio knew a lot more about screenplays than I did—so why not? I told him, though, that the studio would make him change the ending, which would ruin the whole impact of the story. As much as Emilio had been around movies, he still didn't realize how powerless the screenwriter was. There are a lot of good things about that movie, but it turned out to be wishy-washy.

Do you think there will ever be a film version of Taming of the Star Runner?

There might be a film version. One time I did a screenplay for it and got paid, but it's hard, because the book's so in-trospective. As a matter of fact, when I was writing it, I was thinking no one's going to be able to make a movie out of this—two of the major characters are a kid and a cat. But I'm not concerned; I didn't write it to be a movie.

Ultimately, how well do you think the films have complemented your novels?

I'm extremely happy with *Tex* and *Rumble Fish*, because they captured the spirit of the books so well. I'm happy with *The Outsiders* because not only was it a wonderful, wonderful experience for me, it also got recognition for some brilliantly talented boys. And it satisfies my fans. Kids wanted the movie.

You continue to admire good films. Earlier you mentioned Brokeback Mountain. *Why do you think the movie appealed to you so much?*

Brokeback Mountain is one of the first movies I've seen in ages that I've wanted to re-watch and figure out. The director, Ang Lee, made that movie work with his transitions from scene to scene. It's like a piece of literature that resonates in your subconscious. Every time I see it, I see something new. I also re-read books constantly. I re-read all of Jane Austen at least once a year.

Do you see any connection between Brokeback Mountain *and your own stories?*

Not really, except that both are very character-oriented; and I always start with characters. I wanted to see *Brokeback Mountain* because I'd read the short story by Annie Proulx, which blew me away. It's so straightforward and sparse, it grabs your heart. Proulx's metaphors—and some of her dialogue—are incredible. The people who made the movie had the sense to stick with her story.

Have you ever considered developing a property directly for the screen?

Yes, I've written two screenplays, one a paranormal western. If I don't get it made into a movie in a few years, I'm going to novelize it. That's how much I love it. And then I've got another one I developed with my friend Tim Zinneman. I hope to see that get to the screen, too. I've always said writing a novel is like doing an oil painting. You can make it minimalist; you can make it abstract; you can make it photo-realistic. But writing a screenplay is like drawing a coloring book, because other people—set directors, directors, actors—are going to come in and add their shades.

You're still showing up in movies from time to time. What can you tell us about your most recent cameo appearance?

Tim Hunter gave me a call last year—he knew I'd kill to be on the set of a western—and said he was shooting a low-budget western, *The Far Side of Jericho*, in New Mexico. He invited me to visit for week and arranged for me to be an extra. I went to wardrobe and got rigged up as this old ranch woman. I'm still not sure if the movie's going to get released, or if it's going to go straight to video.

Your son, Nick, has become involved in the movie business. What are your hopes for him as he focuses on a medium that has been so gratifying for you?

He hopes to go into film-sound engineering after he graduates. He recently did an internship at George Lucas's Skywalker Ranch and studied film-sound design. All I've ever hoped for Nick is that he'll get into a field, like I did, that he loves. It'll be like getting paid to have fun.

Aleasha: 3/29/91 to 7/31/06

LITTLE KIDS AND VAMPIRES

July 25, 2006—Tulsa, Oklahoma

Susie celebrated her birthday on July 22, and before we get started with our literary talk, she shows me the bronze frogs her husband, David, has given her to celebrate the occasion. Frogs, she tells me, took control of her house several years ago, and now she collects them. The frogs she points out to me in the den are no ordinary frogs; they are art—carefully crafted, colorful, sleek. She has even more frogs in her office, where they inconspicuously line the bookcases and her desk. That's the way she wants it. The frogs aren't imposed on her inner decor; they're carefully placed to be a part of it—and of her ongoing narrative. One frog guards an artificial crow, while another keeps an eye on the Loch Ness monster. Sometimes, Susie says, visitors try to realign the frogs more conventionally, and then she has to put them back into story position.

How was the break you took between your young adult novels and your children's books different from the writer's block you experienced after The Outsiders?

I had a baby, and he was a surprise. He was much wanted, and he was absolutely adored by both his parents. I couldn't take my eyes off him long enough to write anything, and I sure didn't want to write about teenagers.

Why did you decide to return to writing with a children's book?

My editor came to visit me, and we spent all afternoon with the age-old idea sparker, a bottle of scotch. We still couldn't come up with any ideas, so we started sharing kid stories, because his daughter is almost exactly the same age as Nick. I told about this trick that David had played on Nick in kindergarten. Nick came home the first day and said, "Dad, there's a kid in my class that has black hair like you, wears glasses like you, and his name is David like you. Now is that you?" My sensitive, politically correct husband said, "Sure, Nick, that's me. I get little every day and go to school with you." Nick was very puzzled. He thought it wasn't true, but he didn't know for sure. And I have to admit I aided and abetted David. When Nick would come home and say, "Oh, it was so gross today; Kelly threw up," I'd get him ensconced in front of the TV, run and call David, and tell him Kelly had thrown up in class. When David would get home, he'd say, "Nick, weren't you grossed out when Kelly threw up? Ugh!"

What was your editor's response?

I happened to glance over at him, and he seemed torn between falling off the couch laughing and calling the

Department of Human Services. He told me to write the story up, and we'd make it into a children's book. I'd read a lot of children's books to Nick by that time, and I knew what I liked, which was not many words on a page.

What were some of yours and Nick's favorite children's books?

All the Dr. Seuss books. Some of the books I liked as a kid weren't necessarily the ones he liked. I love the Berenstain Bears. Of course, the old standby *Goodnight Moon* is everybody's favorite. The illustrations are just so fantastic.

How did you convert your family story into an actual storybook?

I gave the story a plausible twist, because Nick was pretty clever at that age, too. He'd come home from school and have tests for his dad: "Okay, who lost a tooth today on the playground—was it Colton, was it Sam, was it Rob?" It didn't take long for David to figure out it was always the first name. Nick would always give him three choosements. "Choosements"—I thought that was a good word, so I used "choosements." Another time Nick said, "You know, I have many tricks on my sleeve." So I used that for the ending line.

This was a picture book.

Yes, Random House sent me several books by illustrators they liked, and I got to pick my illustrator, who did very clever illustrations and even managed to put the dog in, even though I had never mentioned the dog. Also, there's a picture of the family sitting on the couch reading, which was very typical of us. Nick said, "You know I'm not redheaded," and David said, "But at least I'm tall," and I said, "And at least I'm skinny."

How involved was the family with the actual writing of the book when you were working on it?

They just listened to it. David got a huge kick out of it, because it was his deal, and it was a true story. We kept it up for almost a year. Nick kind of got a kick out of it because he was going to be in a book. We all three enjoyed it.

Were any of Nick's friends in the book?

Yes. Colton's mom, Sam's mom, and Rob's mom bought the book because their kids' names were in it.

Since you were writing for little kids, did you have to work on softening your characteristic grittiness?

Not my characteristic grittiness. There's not a grit in it. But Nick was mature for his age and had a very sophisticated sense of humor. At times, I may have overestimated other kids' grasp of the situation. I did have to work on that.

Did you have to make any other adjustments as you wrote for a younger audience?

I just had to remember to keep the word count short. I thought I had, but the editor sent it back, saying I needed to cut it even more. He was right. It wasn't a book for children to read; it was a book to read to them. I remember when I was reading books to Nick that I preferred fascinating pictures with a little bit of story.

Was writing text for a picture book ultimately as satisfying for you as writing young adult novels? In other words, did you feel that the picture book was a substantive enough vehicle for your talent?

No, not really. But it was right for that time in my life, because I wasn't ready to get totally involved in writing another novel. I wanted to be creative, but I just didn't have the energy or even the interest to delve into a novel, which takes a whole lot of focus and, for me, a lot of emotional energy.

How closely did you work with the illustrator, Alan Daniel?

We never met, never talked, never e-mailed. But Alan was so clever, including a lot of puns on big and little, tall and short. It almost seemed like he was there with us. In the book, when Nick says he has a question for his mom, that he's just waiting until she finishes her coffee, because she is always nicer—well, that's the way we were. In the illustration, the mom's sitting with her eyes half open, her coffee spilling, just looking at her kid. Somehow Alan knew.

Did you write the book with the idea that the pictures would finish what you were saying?

I hoped the pictures would entertain. And they did. One reason I picked Alan was because I thought his illustrations had a lot of energy to them, even when the characters were just sitting on the couch and reading.

How did the feedback you got from your younger readers compare to the feedback you got earlier in your career?

I have to admit I had no fan letters from five-year-olds. I did have some from adults. My emotional books are the ones that inspire the most fan mail.

You followed Big David, Little David *with* The Puppy Sister, *a chapter book for children. Wasn't this story also based on another real family experience?*

When I got through with *Big David, Little David* and still didn't have any idea what my next novel might be,

Granny, who was Miss Kitty in The Puppy Sister. —S.E.H.

I thought I'd look around the house to see what else I could write about. The Australian shepherd puppy we had brought home to be a sibling for Nick had made herself into a member of the family. I've always been an animal person—as a child I'd make pets out of bugs. But Nick wasn't an animal person, and there was so much sibling rivalry. He'd be going, "Mom, I'm playing Nintendo, and Aleasha's annoying me." Then Aleasha would come running in, like she was saying, "He's supposed to be playing with me!" They finally bonded, and one day, when we came home from a walk, Nick said, "I think Aleasha's wondering when she's going to turn into a real kid like me." And I thought, *There is my hook!*

The fact that Aleasha wants to be a human kid?

Yes, and have more fun like Nick. So through sheer determination, she starts changing herself. I hung the story on a year around the holidays. I figured if Aleasha spent her first year in dog years, she'd be seven by the end of the book. When she finally learns how to talk, Nick gradually breaks it to his parents, and, of course, they're shocked. I think the quote from the book is: "Mom sat down very suddenly on the floor and took a nap." By Halloween, Aleasha's changed enough that she and Nick go out trick-or-treating as werewolves. And then at Christmas, she wakes up, can see colors for the first time, and calls them "smells for the eyes."

That's a great line.

I really like that line, too, even though I did come up with it. By spring Aleasha's become a human girl, goes to a baseball game, then catches a foul ball in her mouth. By the way, she and Nick were still squabbling.

You mentioned in one of our earlier visits that The Puppy Sister *holds the distinction of being the only story, thus far, that you've written from the female perspective. What was it like for you as a storyteller, switching gender and species?*

It was fun. While Aleasha's watching TV, she sees some ballet dancers, stands up on her hind legs, twirls, and turns like a little girl. She has strong toes for ballet—and loves going to lessons—but she can also kick a soccer ball. I'd noticed that Nick and a lot of his friends were into fantasy, imaginative worlds. Their recipes for dragon stew would include lizard eyes and goat blood. But some kids, jocks, were more into their sports, and their recipes for dragon stew were basically potatoes and onions. So Aleasha was the athletic type; Nick was into swordplay.

How did you keep Aleasha from becoming a caricature?

By never thinking of her as a caricature. I used Aleasha's personality as much as I could understand it. She could feel guilty, but then in an instant she chews all of Nick's toys, because she's so mad he's gone off to have fun without her. Which actually did happen in real life with some of Nick's plastic figures. When Nick comes back, Aleasha cowers, saying, "Oh I did it, and I'm so sorry," which, I think, is a dog trait. In the end of the book, the pediatrician, who's been let in on the story, describes her as a perfectly normal little girl, very affectionate and enthusiastic. Aleasha jumps up, grabs Mom around the neck, and says, "I will always be enthusiastic and affectionate—whatever that means."

You speak of your love of animals. Why do you think they play such an important role in your life?

Probably as a child I felt like I could communicate with them better than with the adults in my life or even with my peers. I just always have had a strong communication with animals. There's less pretense.

What can we learn about ourselves by considering how animals like Aleasha might view us?

When we take away an animal's ability to fend for itself, it's up to us to care for it. I had a cat that lived to be over twenty. She came with our house, lived with us for fifteen years, and turned out to be the animal my son bonded with the strongest. Even when she couldn't quite make it to the litter box and couldn't play any more, he could see that she was still a member of the family. We were obligated to take the best care of her we could. In a lot of ways the death of an animal prepares you for dealing with human death. When my horse Toyota died, I was with him until his last minute. The vet said, "Susan, are you sure you want to be here?" And I said, "You're not going to get me away from this horse; the last thing he's going to hear is my voice." Animals teach us responsibility.

What are some of your all-time favorite animal books besides Old Yeller?

When I was in grade school, I absolutely loved *Duff, the Story of a Bear.* I read that book over and over and over. And Marguerite Henry's horse books with those fabulous paintings. *King of the Wind* was one of my favorite books for many years. Then Ernest Thompson Seton's *Wild Animals I Have Known.* He made the point that no animal in the wild dies of old age, so naturally all of his short stories had tragic endings, and the animals were written about just as if they were people. I remember the story about the fox who could raid the hen house until the farmer figured him out. As a younger kid, I loved being outdoors, taking walks through the woods, so wild-animal stories are especially fascinating to me.

In your picture book and your chapter book, you get to display your sense of humor. Was that liberating for you? Your earlier work had some pretty serious overtones.

My sense of humor is one of my strongest personality traits, but—I don't know why—these are the first books where it's really come through. Tex was inclined toward pranks, which I'm not, so even though he had a sense of humor, it was quite different from mine. So it was liberating to get to express that part of myself.

You've already established that Big David, Little David *and* The Puppy Sister *are decidedly autobiographical. At what point does fact become fiction?*

Well, Aleasha didn't turn herself into a real human, but she did turn herself into a member of the family.

Would you agree with Grace Paley that any story told twice is fiction?

That's a good one. Yes, and better for it.

In 2004 you wrote Hawkes Harbor. *Why did you decide to write a book about a vampire?*

I don't really believe in vampires. The vampire actually was more of a character definition. My books show character growth. Jamie Sommers was fearless, but he's in a mental hospital, and one of the first things he tells his doctor is about the time he was smuggling jewels out of Burma, got captured by pirates, jumped into the ocean to save a ruby, and got attacked by a shark. The doctor thinks he's a nut case with an imagination, but his story turns out to be true. Something has happened to break him.

And as if that weren't enough, he meets a vampire.

The vampire, Grenville, was interesting, because I portrayed him as a man who really valued his self-control. For him, being a vampire was like being a drug addict. He couldn't break himself; he wasn't proud of it. But he relished the power that being a vampire gave him.

Did you have any other vampire characters in mind as you wrote the book?

When Grenville and Jamie got together, I was also thinking about the original Dracula and Renfield, the cowering little servant. That whole relationship fascinated me.

Publishers Weekly described the book as "swashbuckling," not exactly what you'd expect for a horror novel.

I felt trapped writing teenage books with drama and meaning—or no meaning—and I wanted to go back to when writing was really fun. I'd just re-read *Treasure Island*, and I had a great time making up Jamie's adventures. After Jamie told his psychiatrist about being in Burma, I went to the globe and saw the Andaman Islands. I looked them up in the dictionary and found out they are beautiful, pristine, but also hangouts for really bad people, so I had Jamie's boat break down near the islands. Then the next issue of *National Geographic* had an article on Burma in the 1960s. The socialist government was collapsing, and two-thirds of the net national income was from smuggling. So many synchronicities kept happening to me while I was writing the book.

Kellen Quinn, Jamie's best friend, is a great character, an Irish con man.

I loved writing his dialogue with Jamie. He had quite a vocabulary, and Jamie was not particularly verbal, but he liked to listen to Kell's stories.

As you just mentioned, much of the book takes place in the 1960s, specifically 1967, the same year The Outsiders *was published. Is that just a coincidence, or was your subconscious at work again?*

My subconscious was at work again, because I realized after I'd written the book that I was using the vampire as a metaphor for the Vietnam draft. People forget how it was. The draft could yank you out of your life, subject you to horrors, then send you back to a country that despised you. Jamie is ripped out of his life by the vampire, subjected to horrors, and driven crazy. The vampire holds him in contempt, but at the end, he and Jamie have gradually learned to respect each other. I actually even mention the Vietnam situation. When Jamie's first sent to the state mental hospital, a lot of Vietnam vets are patients.

The book operates in several different time frames. We've talked about the '60s, but there's an opening prologue dated 1950. Why did you choose the nonlinear structure?

Jamie was a tactile learner. He wasn't a reader, but he liked to work jigsaw puzzles. I realized after I did the book that I was working a jigsaw puzzle. Something will be mentioned in one chapter that will only make sense several chapters later. I think that gives the reader a feeling at the end of having lived a lifetime with somebody.

You've used the name Jamie before with your female character in Tex. *Is there any connection?*

No. I tried to come up with a lot of different names for the character. Jamie just seemed to be the one that suited him.

Horror guru R. L. Stine wrote that he wanted to echo Jamie's plea, "Don't let it be dark." How did that plea originate within you?

I'm not sure. I'm not scared of the dark. I like swimming out in the pool at night by myself. On the surface, Jamie connects the dark with the time the vampire first gets him and torments him. But also Jamie, who was pretty fearless, was in the dark about life. Like when he was running guns with Kell. He was doing a job, getting paid well. It was a little dangerous, but he was totally in the dark about the principle until he realized these guns were going to be used to murder men, women, and children. He's enlightened by the end of the book.

Like Taming the Star Runner, Hawkes Harbor *is written in third person. Was that a calculated decision on your part, or was that just how the story came to you?*

It was calculated. I wanted the freedom in *Hawkes Harbor* to be all over the map, and not just geographically. I was in Burma, I was in Bangkok, I was in the Riviera. Some paragraphs come from the mind of Kell. A few paragraphs come from the mind of the vampire, and from some other characters, too.

You mentioned that this book takes place all over the world, not in Oklahoma like your other books. Why did you decide to shift locales?

Well, I've done Oklahoma to death. I realized later that Jamie and Kell met in Hawaii and kept going farther and farther west. Their first stop was in the Philippines, and then they were in Burma, the French Riviera, Liverpool. It's hot in Burma, but by the end of the book, in Washington, D.C., it's snowing. It's gotten colder and colder and colder. That was an interesting motif.

In Hawkes Harbor *you were writing to an adult audience for the first time in your career. How did that feel?*

I've always wanted to know if I could do sex scenes, and so there are about three in the book. They're not gratuitous;

they're illustrating Jamie's sex education. Kell gets mad at Jamie for buying hookers, because he doesn't need to—he's young; he's good-looking. When he does finally fall in love with a girl, he realizes affection might be the next step.

Many of your fans loved Hawkes Harbor, *but some were uncomfortable with the book. Did that surprise you at all?*

I knew a lot of people would think it was strange. It's funny to me because a lot of people were shocked that there was a vampire in it. I gave plenty of clues, so I didn't think it was going to be any huge surprise when it turned out Mr. Hawkes was not exactly what people thought he was. People seem to have so many ideas about what I'm supposed to be writing, but I've never let anybody dictate what I write. On the other hand, I do get fan mail from people who just loved *Hawkes Harbor*. One woman wrote and said she was in love with Jamie after the first chapter. That was nice. And I think the characters are some of the best I've ever done.

Do you plan on more horror novels, or was Hawkes Harbor *a literary diversion?*

The book I'm working on now is a paranormal suspense comedy—set in Oklahoma.

Do all of your books, as diverse as they are, relate to extended family?

Absolutely. Like the puppy becoming a member of the family, even though she and Nick actually didn't have a whole lot in common. In *The Outsider*s, Ponyboy did not like Dallas in the beginning, but he did admire him by the end of the book. And Grenville and Jamie end up being

family members. Jamie had been searching for a father figure all his life, and he went through several of them—the
priest, Kell, Grenville. All my books are about relationships.

Look at this gorgeous superstar—and Matt's not bad either.—S.E.H.

TIM

The dishwasher is humming in the kitchen as Susie and I admire the framed photo of Matt Dillon riding her horse Toyota. The picture, she tells me, was taken during the filming of Tex, and she's left it on the den coffee table so we can consider it for the book. Matt and Toyota leave little to the imagination. They're not posing. They're naturally young and bold, reined in by the camera, but ready to bolt to a different realm. Susie's also preoccupied with two black-and-white illustrations for Tim's stories, one a work in progress. "This needs to be a little rougher," she says, calling my attention to the image of a worn chair, draped with a banner that reads, "Welcome Home Terry." She goes on to explain that she means rougher like Tim himself, though he's not depicted in the drawings or the stories. The other sketch, featuring a smoldering cigarette, suggests that Tim has just stepped away from the scene for a minute, but, like us, can still hear the dishwasher and see Matt in the distance.

The stories in your collection, Some of Tim's Stories, *focus on Mike and Terry. Who exactly is Tim?*

Tim is the author of the stories. I took a roundabout way of writing in first person, using a narrator who writes his stories in third person. That sounds confusing, but I pictured Tim as a bartender in his late twenties, working in some small northern Oklahoma town. He went to a community college to take computer courses for his job, enrolled in some other courses, got interested in short stories, and decided to write about his life. But he disguised the stories.

How did you get to know him well enough to make him a tangible presence?

I had to establish a strong back story for Tim. The stories are short, so I needed to know every detail of his life. I had to be Tim when I was writing them, and his ideas were totally different from mine. He was not for gun control. He was very, very antiabortion. I'd never felt so masculine in all my life, even though I've always used male narrators and male characters. I even began thinking like a bartender and bouncer. Friday nights are tougher than Saturday nights from the bouncer's point of view because on Fridays people think they deserve their fun—their hard week is over. By Saturday, they're more relaxed. I don't know how I understood that, but I did.

Did you do any research?

I read *Bartending for Dummies* and visited a few bartending sites on the Internet.

How significant is it that Tim's a bouncer as well as a bartender?

The fact that Tim's a bouncer factored into the story because he's not a violent person. Even though he has that potential, he would rather prevent a fight than stop one after it's started.

Did Tim become a presence in your life as well as the stories?

One time when my husband, David, got home, I was telling him what was going on in the bar that night, and he said, "You're starting to sound like him." Tim had a heavy voice, and his words carried weight.

How did you see him physically?

Very strong. He was 6'2". He weighed 185 to 190 pounds. He was big-boned but not heavy. His nose had been broken twice, but because he was heavy-boned, it looked okay. He had a lot of presence to him, even though he was quiet. He always wore a baseball cap, and his customers would bring him caps from the different places they'd been. He had quite a collection. The customers had grown to like him because he was a good listener. He also wore Wranglers—or whatever blue jeans were on sale at Kmart—and Timberland lace-up boots. The boots originally started out mustard-colored, but he had spilled so many things on them they'd turned tan.

Tim never makes even a cameo appearance in the stories. Do you think readers can really get to know him through what he's written?

Definitely. Even though he called his character Mike, he mentions his aunt and his mother and the step-father he refers to as "the step-bastard." Tim had lost his father when he was ten. His father had played a huge role in Tim's life, and I think you can pick that up in the stories, too.

Why was it important for you to filter these stories through Tim?

It was a different narration process, and I enjoy being different sometimes. Because these stories are very short, they are an arc of life, and they mention things repeatedly. Mike—or Tim—carries guilt for not being in prison with his cousin, when he is just as guilty. That guilt shows up even when it doesn't have anything to do with what's happening in a particular story. To me the stories are a novel in a very condensed form.

How is Tim's writing style different from yours?

When I first started writing from Tim's point of view, I was amazed I couldn't do dialogue, because dialogue is my strong point. But dialogue was the hardest part of fiction writing for Tim. In the earlier stories there's not much. But as he got more relaxed with his writing, he got more comfortable using dialogue, too.

Did you ever find yourself slipping out of character and writing as S. E. Hinton?

Not with Tim's stories. I was so involved being that narrator that I found myself being Tim when I should have been S. E. Hinton.

Ever get any Wranglers at Kmart?

Wranglers, no. And I didn't feel any desire to be addicted to Jack Daniel's, which Tim was, or to smoke, or to wear Timberland boots.

How fully did you come to trust Tim as the storyteller?

I trusted him absolutely, because he wasn't writing for publication. He was in love with his creative writing teacher at Tulsa Community College, and that was why he started writing. With her encouragement he got bolder and more fixed in his ideas of what made a story. He wasn't interested in description at all, not as a reader, not as a writer, and yet the stories themselves are very descriptive. He's not saying, "The beautiful green trees by a wonderful blue lake," but he still gives a strong visual for each story.

What are some of his storytelling eccentricities?

He could never hit the apostrophe button, because his big-boned finger always hit the semicolon instead. This doesn't show now because he always went back to polish. When he wrote through the stories the first time, there was no capitalization or punctuation because he just wanted to get them down, and he wasn't fast. A lot of times he wrote stories out in longhand at first because he didn't have a computer at home; he had to wait and use the one at the bar. Also he always used the word "yes," except once or twice he'd say "yep" when he was in conversation, but not "yeah." And there was a finality about the way he would say "yes." I think he got that from his father, who always had that way of saying "yes."

So you knew the whole family, so to speak?

Yes. Tim's mother wasn't a strong woman. When her husband died in a car wreck, she was floundering, married a man she thought would take care of her, and then wasn't strong enough to prevent his abuse of Tim, who left home at seventeen. By the way, Tim finished high school just because the step-bastard said he couldn't.

Of all your first-person narrators, which one is the most like Tim?

None of them even come close.

What about technically speaking? Did you have some of the same challenges writing as Tim that you had writing as Rusty-James in Rumble Fish? *Neither is the gifted observer that Ponyboy is.*

Tim was so much smarter than Rusty-James. He could learn from his mistakes and profit from them—or at least know he'd made them, whether he could control making them again or not. Rusty-James was so oblivious.

But he still isn't a sophisticated storyteller. What is his strength as a writer?

I think the emotional intensity that he brings to his stories. His stories had to start with an emotion.

How did you come up with the premise for the stories, each limited to about a thousand words?

For the heck of it. It's like taking dressage, horseback riding: it's a strong discipline, and it's wearing, but it's an accomplishment when you feel you finally got it right. There are some Zen-like moments. When I first started, I'd think there is no way I'm going to be able to cut a story down to a thousand words, but I'd go back, trim it, then trim it again. In my later stories, I would know I had 995 words without ever looking at my word count.

In our very first interview you said that you'd revised The Outsiders *by adding detail and scenes. How did you pare these stories down to fit the prescribed word length? What sorts of things did you find yourself cutting out?*

You'd be surprised at how much you don't need in a story. I found out you could do without a lot of adjectives. And without a lot of explanation. In "Different Shorelines," the story takes place on a lakeshore at different times of the year and in different years, beginning, I think, in 1987. It's spring, and then you go into summer one year later. But you're always at the same lakeshore, and you don't have to describe it. The conversations explain what's going on.

Do you think that—ironically—in some ways you were able to say more with fewer words?

I think so. Of course, you don't know how to judge your own work, but these short stories are about as vivid as anything I've written.

In our society, we tend to think that shorter is easier. Is that the case with Some of Tim's Stories?

I've always thought longer was easier. That's why I never really got into short stories or poetry. In a novel you have more time to set up what's going on and to explore. Tim's stories are a little easier, because they revolve around the same characters in Tim's life. I didn't have to start a whole new premise with each story. Each one can stand alone as a short story. But when you finish, you'll have the feel of a novel.

Why did you decide against writing a frame for the stories that explains the Tim connection and the story format?

Because it's such a delicate balance. I could pretend that I met Tim or that his creative writing teacher gave me his stories, but to me that would ruin the concept. I think the observant reader will figure out why they're called Tim's stories. I just didn't want to mess with them. They're rugged—like old pieces of granite—but the thread that holds them together is delicate.

How important, then, is the actual sequence of the stories?

I wrote them at completely different times. It wasn't until I was through that I decided on the order. But I wanted to develop a time mark so that one story could help explain another. When you read "Sentenced" and Mike's aunt mentions his old girlfriend, he says, "I don't see her anymore." Then you realize that in the previous story, "The Girl Who Loved Movies," Amber is the girl. There's a later story where Mike's talking about a memory he had from childhood, when he heard his dad having a nightmare, but it turns out it's really about Mike/Tim being in love with this other woman. By the placement of the story, you can see she was his creative writing teacher. These aren't flashbacks; they're memory stories.

In many ways your writing style in these stories reminds me of Elmore Leonard's. I know you've read his western novels. What literary influence do you think guided your approach to this collection?

Of course, you like to think of yourself as influence-free, but even Homer was influenced by somebody. So, probably Hemingway. I've got tons of biographies about him; he's an absolutely fascinating character. You couldn't make up this man. But his short stories are the only writings of his that I really admire, and I think—probably—his spare style influenced me.

In "Class Time," Mike has read Hemingway's To Have and Have Not. *Is that one of your favorites?*

I'd always heard *To Have and Have Not* was one of Hemingway's worst books. But when I was taking a movie class just a few years ago, we studied the film version, and I finally read the novel. I thought it was great. That'll teach me to listen to other people's opinions! Mike also mentions that he can't read Henry James. I enjoy Henry James.

You've often said that you re-read Jane Austen's work about once every year. What have you learned from reading her novels that's made you a better writer?

Her revelation of character through dialogue is just fascinating, and that's what I do best.

In many ways, Mike and Terry are reminiscent of your earlier characters. How do they transcend those roles?

I might be reverting. We talked about this earlier—one of my closet relationships when I was growing up was with my cousin, Jimmy. We were raised like brother and sister. We did everything together—skied, fished, played football. Our families were always with each other. That bond is even stronger with Mike and Terry, because they're double first cousins. Their fathers are brothers, and their moms are sisters. They have the same backgrounds and are bound together, but they're certainly not the same people.

You've already mentioned Tim's mom and her weakness. In the book Aunt Jelly is a remote but powerful presence. Would you agree that she's one of your most fully realized characters?

Yes, but I go back and forth between calling her "Aunt Jelly" and "Julie." "Jelly" is obviously a childhood nickname for her. She was probably always making the boys jelly sandwiches. I have an aunt Eloise (that's my middle name) who was called "Peeny" because she always liked "peeny" butter sandwiches. Aunt Jelly is a strong woman, except that she spoils Terry. She'd like to spoil Mike, but he won't let her. He's the responsible one. One of the lines in the stories says it best: Mike's step-father's resentment was probably no worse than Terry's mom's indulgence.

Do you think you, aka Tim, have taken your initial themes to a new level through these characters?

Maybe so. They're not outsiders. In *Hawkes Harbor*, Grenville was an outsider and so was Jamie to a certain degree. Only at the end of the book did Jamie realize that the townspeople accepted him as another citizen. Tim's stories are about how your environment and your own personality shape your life. Tim has a drinking problem, but he doesn't take any steps to rectify it, even though he knows he should. In his environment, his drinking is accepted. Terry's the one who doesn't drink, and he gets in the most trouble.

What could you say as a mature writer through Tim that you couldn't say as a teenager through Ponyboy?

Tim/Mike has a lot of hard-earned wisdom. Ponyboy can be wise, but he's an idealistic kid who still thinks the world can be changed. Tim knows the world's not going to change, but he's trying to figure out how to deal with it. As a bartender he realizes that when people come into the bar and pour out their stories to him, he's not there to fix their lives. As he puts it, he's not a social worker, but he figures out what people want to hear from their bartender, and he decides that's what he needs to give them. In a way, that's a cop-out. The name of that story, by the way, is "What's Your Poison?"

You've also adapted many of these stories as plays. How did placing your characters in a different format give you new insights into them and their circumstances?

I don't know, but it was very interesting to do. I had to figure out how to work with Mike, Tim, and Terry as three separate people. I gave Mike the on-stage ability to do narration. Tim was off to the side in the same clothes writing the story.

I wonder if casting the stories as plays also gave you a better sense of dialogue—maybe even timing. As you've pointed out, Tim had to struggle with dialogue.

I don't ever have to think about dialogue consciously.

Which of Tim's stories stand out as favorites of yours?

"The Girl Who Loved Movies" is my favorite. It's the shortest story, but it's one of the strongest. I think of it as a metaphor that can stand by itself. I also like "Visit," when Mike finally comes to visit Terry. And "The Missed Trip." In that story, Mike as an adult is contemplating what would have happened if their fathers, both his and Terry's, hadn't been killed in a car wreck together. He feels pretty ashamed of his life at that point. He's in his mid-twenties—in a do-nothing job—and Terry's in prison.

In "The Girl Who Loved Movies," you have this great closing line: "It was cliché he knew. But he meant it classic." Did you know how lyrical those words were the moment you wrote them or did you have to wait for the initial feedback from your early readers?

I did know. I wrote that whole story in just a few hours, realizing that was going to be my ending line.

In fact your closing lines are stunning throughout the collection. Do you think the shorter format called upon you to create more emphatic endings?

Yes, I do. The only open-ended story in the book is the last one, "No White Light No Tunnel," but it's still a closed chapter in Tim's mind. Some of the stories are even funny, like when Mike/Tim finally managed to get Terry worried about something in "Full Moon Birthday." I get very upset with a book that doesn't have a strong ending, and it was almost an indulgence to have this many strong endings to work toward.

Strong endings, yes, but there's still a sense of the stories being ongoing.

Some of the stories are unresolved, but, at their moment in time, I think they are definite. Terry didn't come home from prison and adjust immediately; Mike just hopes in the end that the old Terry is still there. And with "The Girl Who Loved Movies," in my mind, I picture Mike looking up Amber again. But I'm not going to write a sequel. Why press my luck here?

How significant do you think Tim's stories are in your overall career as a writer?

They're the best writing I've ever done. They may be the best writing I'll ever do. Who knows? You always think the next book's going to be the best one, unless you're writing something like *Hawkes Harbor*, which was such self-indulgent fun. But I do think these stories are going to stand the test of time and will end up being mentioned as some of my best work.

What lasting impact do you think Tim will have on you personally and professionally?

Professionally I hope the stories will give people a broader insight into my writing. I don't pigeonhole myself, so it would be nice if readers could get over the fact—a little bit—that I wrote *The Outsiders*. I'm hoping *Some of Tim's Stories* will do well critically, but they're done. I don't plan to revisit them, but I do miss Tim sometimes.

I was going to ask about that, because you were so close to him.

Tim's like somebody I knew once. He used to come over and tell me what was going on, not just stories, but about people getting into fights and about ladies who wanted him to walk them to their cars, supposedly for tip money but, as it turned out, not for money at all. It was really interesting being privy to that life.

You made publishing history as a teenager. What do you still have to accomplish as a writer?

I always want to write a better book; I always want to write another book. I can't do anything else. I also want to feel productive and useful in my life, but I never think in terms of what I've got to accomplish. I don't compete with *The Outsiders*. It's there; I'm proud of it, but I'm through with it, like I am with Tim's stories.

How would you sum up your career so far?

I've been lucky in a lot of ways. Luck got me my agent, Marilyn, or was it coincidence, synchronicity? But luck didn't sell *The Outsiders*—or the other books. I've worked hard.

Have you ever felt like writing was a responsibility?

To a certain degree. I was given a gift, and it's my duty to use it in the best way I can. I don't want to throw it back in God's face. But the fact that I enjoy writing makes everything kind of easy.

Interviewer Teresa Miller is the editor of the Oklahoma Stories & Storytellers series and host of public television's *Writing Out Loud*. She is also the founder and executive director of the Oklahoma Center for Poets and Writers. Her writings include novels *Remnants of Glory* and *Family Correspondence*. She resides in Tulsa, Oklahoma.